What
goes around,
comes around

What goes around, comes around

Published by The Conrad Press Ltd. in the United Kingdom 2023

Tel: +44(0)1227 472 874

www.theconradpress.com

info@theconradpress.com

ISBN 978-1-915494-32-0

Typesetting and Cover Design by: Charlotte Mouncey, www.bookstyle.co.uk

The Conrad Press logo was designed by Maria Priestley.

Printed and bound in Great Britain by Clays Ltd, Elcograf S.p.A

What goes around, comes around

S. J. Roach

List of Characters

Family

Marian Ellershaw Tay	Mother
Hubert Ellershaw	Father (deceased)
Robert Tay	Stepfather
Willie and Lena Catlow	Maternal grandparents
Grandma Ellershaw	Paternal grandma
Uncle Tony	Paternal uncle
Cousin Betty	Cousin
Uncle John	Betty's father
Auntie Elsie	Betty's mother
Ellen	Cousin
Drew	Family friend

Junior School

Mr Hall	Headmaster
Ann Littlewood	Friend
Lynne Wilkinson	Friend
Carry Briton	Friend
Anna Hartley	Friend
Mary Birch	Friend
Jane Harvey	Friend

BRANTHAM GRAMMAR SCHOOL

Harriet (Harry) Bowen   Best friend

Bernadette Morrow

Belinda Rudd

Pippa Jones

Penny Hodge

Eva Brand   Narrator of story

Joan Digby

Jean   Pig farmer's daughter

Charlotte Jackson

Isobel   Head prefect at Moonacre

Lynn Barton

Rose Parker

Craig   Pippa Jones' boyfriend

Miss Rayne   Games mistress

Miss Carter   Housemistress at Moonacre

Mr Grey   Teacher outdoor activities

Joss Wright   Headmaster

Peg Wright   Headmistress

Miss Livingstone   Cook at Moonacre

Barry   Head boy

BOYFRIENDS

Pete	School
Tony Sands	Local boy
Eddie	School
Geoff	Stoke-on-Trent
Frankie	Navy - Cornwall
Ricky	Mod
Phillip	Eva's boyfriend
Fred	Farmer and Harry's boyfriend
Jack and Chris	Eva's brothers

MATRONS

Miss Cross	Moonacre
Miss Bea	Ford House

OTHER

Police Constable Horn	Brantham Village
Natasha	Friend in Cornwall

Chapter 1

I watched Rebecca Ellershaw from a distance, always at a distance. I admired her and wanted to be just like her. She was such fun – dynamic and a daredevil. I was quiet, timid, and always blushed embarrassingly whenever anyone paid attention to me. I so wanted to be able to laugh and flirt with others just like she did.

That was then!

'Have you got your skipping rope with you today, Rebecca?' asked little Cary Briton, a petite child, who was the same age as Rebecca at seven years.

'I always have it, Cary, you know that!' Rebecca bit back sharply.

It was widely known that Rebecca Ellershaw was the best skipper in the infant and junior school at Heasandford and Cary always felt a sense of pride when it was her time to turn the rope for her. Rebecca could 'pepper 'and 'do the bumps' better than anyone and always won the skipping competitions at playtime.

It was the mid-1950s in the north west of England where the small red brick-built school with the green, spiked railings nestled amongst the dark stone back-to-back terraced houses. The stone had turned a dirty grey colour due to the black bellowing smoke from the tall chimneys of this industrial northern town. Each household burned the dense black stuff, known as coal, in their small fireplaces, adding to the smoke-filled air.

It was the only way for the cotton mill workers and the miners of this working community to heat their homes. There was no central heating back then – well, not for the likes of these simple mill folk.

Rebecca was an only child. Her mother, Marian Ellershaw, was widowed when Rebecca was six months old. Rebecca's father, Hubert, had died as a result of his war wounds. He was injured on the beaches of Dunkirk and had never fully recovered.

It was a very sad time for the Ellershaws, Marian being a widow at such a young age and having a baby to care for. But they were very fortunate to have the loyal support of Marian's parents, Grandpa and Grandma Catlow – who both worked nearby in one of the several cotton weaving mills of Lancashire – with whom they lived and where Rebecca was born.

It was a substantial house at the end of a large, terraced block. There were three large bedrooms and an upstairs bath-room with a sink. In those days the toilet was a small shed-type structure in the back yard. Other similar houses had a block of toilets at the end of their long back gardens which were communal. So, in hindsight the Catlows could be called posh, having their own private toilet for their household.

Grandpa and Grandma Catlow owned this house having paid five hundred pounds for it just after they were married. They were amongst the lucky ones for it was very rare for a mill worker to own his or her own home.

Rebecca was her grandparents' pride and joy; she could do no wrong. Her mum, Marian, worked hard as a seamstress and worked from home so she was always there when Rebecca returned from school. She was very thankful for her trade even though at times it was hard to make ends meet.

She spent long hours making individual garments for her many customers, but it was a living and Rebecca could have all her clothes made to her own design; when time allowed, that is.

There was little time for socialising away from the family; Grandma made sure of that. She was a very strict lady. Grandpa was the quiet one. Marian definitely took after her dad as she was a gentle lady with high standards. Someone once said, 'Marian's cup is always half full, never half empty.' She remained a decent kindly lady all her life.

Rebecca never liked being left alone. She would rebel whenever Marian went out in the evening to attend her pottery-painting class at the local night school with her old friends or, on the rare occasion, when she attended the local dance hall.

'That child's been crying for you all night since you went out, Marian,' Grandma scolded, 'You should be here taking care of her, not gallivanting all over town.'

'Once this month I've been out, Mum, that's all. What else can I do?'

'She doesn't like you leaving her, poor child,' Grandma replied.

Marian tended to ignore her mother's remarks, thinking that things were better left unsaid. One would never get the last word with Grandma Catlow. *Anything for a quiet life* thought Marian.

Although she thought her parents were the best, Marian often dreamed of a way to escape this Victorian household, but they were only dreams, she supposed.

Rebecca knew, even at that age, that Grandma and Grandpa would always be her loyal supporters and she would usually get her own way, whatever the circumstances. School was different however; there Rebecca had to compete with others. She realised at a young age she was not academically gifted, although her position within the class of about forty pupils was just below halfway. It's fair to say she struggled with mathematics but was quite good at writing and compositions and it was a dream when she was awarded the merit badge, a weekly award at junior school, for her one hundred per cent score in her fractions.

It was an accolade to receive this badge amongst the young pupils when each Friday afternoon, one pupil from each class would make the walk up onto the stage in front of the whole school to be presented with the badge by the then headmaster Mr Hall.

Rebecca received the merit badge on one occasion only.

Anna Hartley and Mary Birch were in the same class. They were bright girls, slightly rough around the edges, with strong personalities. I suppose you could say they had a tendency to bully lesser individuals. They were bossy and intimidated Rebecca to let them play with her skipping rope. She always let them have their way to avoid further trouble, but she resented them to the point at which she felt like boiling over.

They never bullied Mary's friend Jane Harvey. She was a

blonde, petite girl whom everyone liked. She was good at ballet and starred in local productions in the town. Everyone wanted to play with Jane; even Rebecca. She wanted to be like her and felt clumsy next to her. Jane always sat at the back of the class; Rebecca was always at the front. The higher in the class you were academically, the further towards the back you could sit. So, Rebecca never sat next to Jane!

Just wait until playtime, they will all want my skipping rope and want me to turn it for them, she thought. Rebecca was good at that. The other girls were also amazed at how long Rebecca could skip the bumps, sometimes thirty or forty, one after the other, until she was truly exhausted. And the rope never caught her out. Rebecca had had enough of the intimidation and bullying especially by Anna Hartley. It was time to show her a thing or to. She waited until PE time when all the children changed into their shorts and tee-shirts and then she carefully unpinned the merit badge from the cardigan of Anna Hartley. She secreted it in her coat pocket. Satisfied with this, she changed into to her own PE kit and joined her class.

Later, there was a search by the class all around the playground, to look for the badge, which it was felt must have fallen off the cardigan at playtime. It was the first time she had seen Anna Hartley cry.

No one found the badge.

It was devastating for Rebecca not to qualify for the class trip.

Being in the top twenty-four in the class test was the decider. Rebecca was twenty-fifth. She could only go if another pupil dropped out. That didn't happen; she was out of luck.

Grandma comforted her, 'We will go by coach to the Lake District, Rebecca, and tour the seven lakes.' But that was no comfort, she felt completely worthless. *Everything would be fine if I was up there nearer the top*, she thought. Sadly, she never reached those dizzy heights, always remaining near the bottom; but she was never last.

Generally though, Rebecca's time at Heasandford Junior School was a happy one. She looked forward to meeting Grandpa on her way home from school at dinner time. She would call at the Bishop's Street weaving mill and wait at the end of Grandpa's looms where he worked. The clatter of the looms in the weaving mill was absolutely deafening. Rebecca always stood there with her fingers in her ears and watched the mill workers mouthing instructions and chatting silently to one another. It looked very funny watching them, with their hand movements trying to make themselves understood.

Then the hooter would sound, a deafening high-pitched scream, which was heard above all the noise of the clattering looms. The mill workers would stop their looms immediately, silence... then the place emptied, the shift all going home for their dinner with dawn in their hair (white fluff from the cotton). The dawn didn't stay too long on Grandpa's head, as he was a bit thin on top, with a comb-over. Grandpa and Rebecca walked up the main road together, like peas in a pod, He was so special to her – the best – making her laugh at his silly jokes and stories of when he was a comedian in Blackpool Tower Circus, when he was a young man.

Rebecca was at her happiest with Grandpa and always looked forward to walking back to Barbon Street with him at dinner times for one of Grandma's proper dinners. They didn't have much time to eat it though as they had to walk back down the road again for Grandpa had to return to the mill and Rebecca to school.

She never looked forward to the walk home at four o'clock. She used to meet her cousin Ellen who, for some reason, didn't seem to like her. Ellen used to tell her she was going to beat her up and put her in a dustbin. The two girls would meet, unintentionally, at the junction of Queen Victoria Road and Briercliffe Road, Ellen having walked from her school, St John's, and Rebecca from Heasandford. It seemed to Rebecca that Ellen was deliberately waiting for her. That dreaded feeling in the pit of Rebecca's stomach was always there. Ellen would block Rebecca's way home and wouldn't let her pass on the pavement, pushing and shoving her.

She was from a large family with five brothers and a sister. Her father and Rebecca's father were brothers. The families didn't seem to get together for social occasions, which seemed very strange to Rebecca, as she was an only child and would have loved to play with her cousins, but it never happened. But boy, was she glad it never did, as the dislike for Ellen intensified inside Rebecca. *One day, Ellen Ellershaw, my time will come!* she thought, *what goes around comes around*, as Grandma Catlow always said.

It was 1958 and the three friends, Rebecca, Anne Littlewood, and Lynne Wilkinson who all lived on Barbon Street and went to Heasandford Junior School, stood in awe as they looked up at Rebecca's grandma's chimney.

'It's an aerial,' Anne spoke excitedly. 'Rebecca, you must have a new television. How exciting! Can we come in and see it?'

The three friends ran as fast as they could; this was probably the first television in the street and they were so excited. Now they could watch all the programmes they had heard so much about.

'Where are you three running to in such a hurry?' It was Ellen, Rebecca's cousin. She spoke in a menacing way.

The girls stopped and said nothing. Then, the pushing started and Rebecca fell back against the gable end wall of the house in Killington Street, hurting the back of her head against the stone wall.

'Tell me what you are doing and what's going on!' Ellen insisted. The other two girls were frightened.

'She's got a new telly at her house. We're all going to watch *Children's Hour*,' they timidly answered.

'Well, I'm coming too, I want to see it, I haven't got one at my house. I'll be watching your telly now,' Ellen replied.

Rebecca was angry. She didn't cry, crying is for babies. *This will not happen again*, she promised herself. She regained her composure and walked up to Ellen until their faces nearly touched one another. Ellen wasn't expecting what happened next as Rebecca pulled Ellen's head back by her long ponytail. With her grandma's scissors, which she had taken from the kitchen drawer that morning, already in her hand, she held the girl down backwards and cut off her long ponytail in one snip. Rebecca threw the hair onto the ground and kicked it into the gutter of the cobbled street.

Screams and tears came from cousin Ellen and she was left speechless at Rebecca's words:

'That's for all the times you've bullied me and made me cry. You will not be watching my television, ever, so there, cry baby.'

The three little girls carried on their way to Rebecca's house and watched the Ecco television for the first time.

'I knew Grandma's scissors would come in handy one day!' she remarked to her friends.

It wasn't long before the two Barbon Street friends let it be known to the class at school of Rebecca's antics with her cousin. No more was she intimidated or approached to hand over her skipping rope. In fact, it became, 'Rebecca, can we play with you?' or 'Will you turn the rope for us?'

'Get your own rope!' was the reply to Anna Hartley and Mary Birch. She would never turn the rope for them again. Back at home it had been worth getting a few slaps across the legs from her mother, especially when her grandma sympathised with her, stating that Rebecca must have been provoked in order to do such a wicked thing.

Rebecca never gave it another thought and also never replaced the scissors back in grandma's kitchen drawer!

CHAPTER 2

Scorpio is the star sign for those born in early November. They say scorpions have a sting in their tale. Rebecca Ellershaw was born on the 13th November 1950. Always smiling and laughing and great fun to be with, of that, there was no doubt, until such times when things didn't always go her way.

Life, as in any northern household, was ordinary. Weekends were always family affairs, with aunts and uncles visiting and staying for one of Grandma Catlow's sumptuous Sunday teas. No expense was spared at her table; there were always plenty of goodies, meats, fine desserts, cakes and biscuits, all homemade by Grandma and Marian.

No one ever refused an invitation to tea at Grandma Catlow's home. Rebecca loved having all her relations visiting, especially two of her other cousins. They were marvellous to be with; cousin David and cousin Betty who were much older that Rebecca. She was totally spoilt by all her relations and thought this was just how it should be, getting chocolate and sweets on each of their visits, especially at Easter when the Easter eggs stood majestically in a long row on the top of Grandpa's piano.

This routine was the norm each weekend. Occasionally, the Catlows would visit Grandma Ellershaw and Uncle Tony and other aunties and uncles. They took it in turns to make the Saturday and Sunday tea, but as we all know, nothing ever stays the same. Things always move on; sometimes for the better and sometimes not.

The information the Catlows received from their daughter Marian, when Rebecca was about nine years of age, wasn't entirely welcomed. It took them a long time to process this new knowledge as it came out of the blue, totally unexpected.

They had built their lives around Marian and Rebecca ever since Hubert had died and it would be very strange for them not to be living together under the same roof.

Marian had met a young man at a local dance. His name was Robert Tay. He lived at the other end of the town in a more affluent area with his elderly mother and her sister. Robert and Marian had been keeping company for a number of weeks, meeting only on a Tuesday evening as it was difficult for Marian to leave the house without causing suspicion. But this arrangement grew tiresome for this outspoken young gentleman and he persuaded Marian to tell her parents of their relationship.

Reluctantly, Marian did so. It wasn't an easy thing to do, nor was it an easy thing for the Catlows to hear. However, the situation had to be accepted by them because it was time Marian had her own life with male friends included in it. It was also time for Marian to introduce Rebecca to Robert Tay, if they were to spend more time together. It was important this was done carefully. Marian knew Rebecca was a strong-willed child and equally, Robert Tay was not used to children, having lived with his mother and aunt all his life. And he was not the easiest person to win over.

A task ahead, it would seem!

Rebecca gazed up at the man dressed in a grey suit; *very grand*, she thought, *looks rich, wonder if he has a car?*

Robert Tay wasn't a bad-looking man in his thirties, six feet tall, of medium build with a grey mop of hair. Marian told Rebecca he worked in the office next to the pet shop near to where they were standing.

'How are you, Rebecca? It's good to finally meet you at last, I've heard a lot about you,' he said, with a broad beam across his face. He had a dimple in his chin.

Marian's cheeks were flushed pink. *Maybe she isn't well*, Rebecca thought. He invited Marian and Rebecca to the cinema. *What, go with those two?* she pondered. *Why would I want to do that? Why would Mum want to go to the cinema with him?*

'Mr Tay is the manager of a coach company in town, Rebecca, and he wants us to go to the cinema with him. Would you like that?'

'What film?' Rebecca asked.

'It's called *South Pacific*, you'll enjoy it. It's all about sunny islands and deep blue seas on the other side of the world,' Marian explained.

Well, I'll go, Rebecca thought, *but I'll be sitting between them; he'll not holding my mummy's hand!*

Rebecca had not seen deep blue seas before, only the sea at Ilfracombe and Worthing which wasn't always blue. This was when she was on holiday with all the family, including the aunts, uncles, and cousins.

She had been to Blackpool sands before and ridden on the donkeys but the sea was always a dirty grey colour. *So maybe*

I'll give South Pacific a go. It will be something different anyway, she admitted to herself.

Rebecca didn't really warm to this man and apparently nor did Grandpa and Grandma but they had to accept the situation and hoped nothing further would develop between this gentleman and their daughter. They could most likely see big changes coming and it was unthinkable for Grandma and Grandpa to lose their only daughter and granddaughter to this man who lived on the other side of town. But she went to the cinema anyway.

Mr Tay collected them from Grandma's in his big black car. It had running boards along each side of it. Grandma stood on the doorstep, still in her 'pinnie' which she always wore at the mill and waved them off.

'We won't be late, Mum,' Marian called to Grandma Catlow.

'Better not be. That child should be in bed at a decent time,' she replied.

Grandpa Catlow didn't say much. He remained in the house reading the sports page of his *Daily Express*; trivial matters didn't interest him. He looked forward to the sport on a Saturday on his new telly and the build-up to it.

Rebecca sat in the back of the large car on the long, black leather seat. Each time the car turned a corner or rounded a bend she slid along the seat to the other end. It was a most uncomfortable ride, *much better to be on the bus*, she thought.

'This is a big car, Mr Tay, is it yours?' Rebecca asked smugly.

'Don't asked rude questions, Rebecca,' Marian spoke curtly to her daughter. She felt very embarrassed by such a question.

The car was on loan to Robert Tay from a work colleague and he wished the smart little missy would just keep quiet. Rebecca slid about on the seat the whole journey to the cinema. *He's probably doing it on purpose*, thought Rebecca, *well, there is no way this man is sitting next to my mummy in the pictures. I will be sitting in between them and we will not be sitting on the back row. That's where all the couples kiss and cuddle.* She couldn't understand why her mummy wanted to go out with this man whom they didn't really know.

The Odeon cinema was a large, art deco style building in the centre of the town. Behind it was a large, rough makeshift car park where the ground was unmade with a covering of old black cinders. It was a bad, cold, and rainy evening and there were several puddles in the car park. This is where Robert Tay parked the car.

'Mack the Knife' by Bobby Darin was playing as they all three entered the cinema, looking like the perfect family sitting together in a row, in front of the big screen. Rebecca sat between them so there would be no holding hands. She was very satisfied she had kept them apart and was looking forward to the film and seeing the blue sea of the faraway places, not to mention an ice lolly in the interval.

It was a long, though very enjoyable film. Rebecca loved it all – the story and the songs. She would like to see it all again. In fact, it was definitely her 'very favourite film', she said later to her mum.

The time in the cinema went very quickly and she enjoyed her ice lolly, but soon it was time to leave. It was dark, wet, and cold outside and the rain had caused several black puddles to appear in the uneven surface of the car park. The car was parked right in the middle of a huge puddle, *but never mind, we will be home in no time at all. Then we will be rid of him*, she thought.

Rebecca knew she must thank Mr Tay for this treat to the cinema but did not do so at once. She thanked him only when she knew she and her mum would have to get the bus home.

The car had a flat tyre which was directly in the middle of a puddle. It was going nowhere soon. However, Rebecca and her mum had to get home and left Mr Tay to change the wheel himself. They really had to get home on the last bus, otherwise Grandma would be livid. It was late as it was.

'Thank you for taking us to the cinema, Mr Tay,' Rebecca said sweetly, with a smirk across her face.

'Poor Mr Tay,' Marian said, 'He'll get wet through and get all his smart suit filthy on that wet ground. Come on, Rebecca, we will have to make that last bus.

CHAPTER 3

Grandma Ellershaw and Uncle Tony were the mother and brother of Rebecca's late father. They arrived for tea at the Catlow home on Saturday afternoons every alternate week. The two grandmas had always been friendly but never referred to each other by their first names. It was always Mrs Ellershaw and Mrs Catlow.

Rebecca thought that was very funny and Grandpa and she always giggled at them when they were in a conversation. Uncle Tony had never married, but apparently had held a soft spot for Marian after she was widowed on account of his brother Hubert dying.

Mealtimes were a great occasion for the two families as there were always good, fresh meats, and vegetables, followed by Grandma's home baking of fruit pies and puddings. It was the same at Grandma Ellershaw's house. Uncle Tony was a professional baker so the food was equally scrumptious.

Willie Catlow was never perturbed by the stream of visitors to his home in Barbon Street. As long as he could check the pool draws on his Littlewoods coupon, he was more than happy. On checking the draws, there was usually a 'damn' and a 'blast' uttered when the scores didn't go his way, but happily, no stronger language, otherwise Grandma Catlow would have given him a clout o'er th' ear 'ole, with the back of her hand or a rolled-up newspaper, but all in good fun.

Wonder what Grandma Ellershaw and Uncle Tony have brought me today? thought, Rebecca. They never came empty-handed but had started bringing nutty sweets with a crisp coating and Rebecca was not keen on them. She whispered this to her mum. Grandma Ellershaw overheard the conversation and wasn't best pleased. She was upset by Rebecca's comments, but it didn't really worry Rebecca. *At least Grandma Ellershaw won't buy those sweets anymore*, was her only thought.

A lot of the conversation that day was about Mr Tay whom Grandma Ellershaw had known since he was a small boy as they had lived close to each other. Rebecca heard the conversation between the adults. Grandma Ellershaw didn't appear to be too happy that her daughter-in-law was keeping company with Robert Tay.

'Always had chapped or chafed legs as a young boy; his fat thighs rubbed together when he ran. I remember him as a rude boy,' added Grandma Ellershaw.

It was easy for Rebecca to eavesdrop on the conversation between her two grandmas and Uncle Tony as she played with her dollies under the large, rectangular, oak table which was already set for the Saturday tea. She was so pleased that they didn't seem to like him, nor did she.

To share her mummy with him was unthinkable but *Grandma and Grandpa wouldn't let that happen, would they?*

Grandma Ellershaw and Uncle Tony doted on Rebecca and it is easy to understand why. Rebecca was born six months before Hubert died from an injury he received in the Second World

War on the beaches of Dunkirk and this eventually caused his premature death. According to records, Hubert placed his helmet over a hand grenade which fell on the beach in front of him and his East Lancashire Regiment. He covered the helmet with his body and the device exploded injuring his legs and left hand causing the amputation of two fingers. He was lucky to survive but sadly only for a few more years.

Rebecca could do no wrong in Grandma Ellershaw's and Uncle Tony's eyes and was always the centre of attention when they were around, applauding her when she sang for them. That was the evening's entertainment whenever they visited.

Robert Tay slowly played a bigger part in Marian's life. The incident at the cinema must not have put him off, much to Rebecca's disappointment. She and her mum would sometimes visit him at his house which he shared with his mother and his auntie on the other side of town. It was a nice house; one of a block of four, with two bedrooms, a bathroom and toilet upstairs which pleased Rebecca. She hated going out into the back yard at Grandma's and Grandpa's when it was cold and wet. This was much more convenient.

His mother and auntie were nice old ladies and treated Marian and Rebecca well. She enjoyed her visits with them but was glad to go home again in the evening, away from Mr Tay, as she still didn't really care for him.

It came as a shock to all the family when Marian announced she was going to marry Robert Tay. She had thought long and hard about the situation. Although it was hard to leave her parents, Marian wanted a new life for herself, and a father for

Rebecca. She was still a young widow and life had to go on. She was sure she was doing the right thing.

The extended family seemed to have accepted him as he had visited them when they were on family holidays to Ilfracombe and Worthing and, sure enough, on the 7th May 1960, at Habergam Church, the two were married.

Rebecca and cousin Betty were bridesmaids, both wearing smart summer suits and carrying matching handbags. Rebecca had her first Cuban heel shoes and felt very grown up. All the family attended, including Mr Tay's family, some of them who lived in London. They all seemed to be having a good time. In fact, it seemed a very happy occasion.

Something that did pray on Rebecca's mind: she now had a different surname from that of her mother. She didn't like that, nor the marriage, but knew she had to make the best of the whole situation because she could do nothing about it.

'A new daddy', Marian had told her, but Rebecca still didn't feel right about this turn of phrase. No one was going to force her into calling him 'Dad' or 'Daddy', not even her mummy. The only person close to a daddy was Grandpa, he had always been there for her. Now she had to leave him and go and live with another man who was acting at being her daddy.

The new family lived in Mr Tay's house. His mother and auntie moved to an elderly person's small bungalow, a short walk away. Rebecca had her own bedroom, which was good, and she made new friends in the area which was also good. She remained at the same school and travelled across town on her new Dawes Daisy Bell cycle which Mr Tay had bought her. It was quite a journey for a ten-year-old, but Rebecca had passed her cycling proficiency test and had the certificate and badge to show for it, so all was well.

CHAPTER 4

Rebecca Ellershaw Tay was not too bad a name and Rebecca agreed to the adoption by Mr Tay. Her reasoning for this was that she wanted the same name as her mother; that was only right and the only reason she agreed. A new birth certificate was issued and all the legalities dealt with. She was now officially Rebecca Ellershaw Tay.

The eleven-plus exam loomed. Rebecca had some private lessons in mathematics, a subject she found difficult. All she wanted was to be able to attend the same high school as cousin Betty and wear the high school's brown blazer with pride. Sadly, this was not to be. Rebecca surprisingly failed the examination. The only school she was going to now was the all-girls school, on the other side of town. She really didn't want to go there and let her mother and Robert Tay know this. As far as Rebecca was concerned this was not going to happen.

However, it was a long time until September, when the new school year would begin and all Rebecca had in her mind was the long summer holidays which stretched out before her.

Holidays with the whole family had now ceased, Robert Tay and Marian were now married and they would have their holidays, just the three of them. This year it was a long car ride down to Cornwall. They would set off at about midnight as the traffic would be lighter and they would arrive reasonably early the next day. They were touring and spending different nights at guest houses in the county. Travelling from one guest house to another was all very exciting, never knowing where you would be sleeping that night.

Rebecca liked Perranporth with its large sandy beaches, and the weather was very hot. Her mum would rub sun cream on Rebecca so she wouldn't burn when she was running in and out of the sea. Marian wore her bathing costume, but Mr Tay only took his shirt off. He never wore shorts and continually wore old-fashioned, open, brown leather sandal, with his socks on. He wasn't very modern.

The guest house in Perranporth was a very large Victorian terrace, painted red with whitewashed walls reflecting the sun. It was a very pretty-looking property. Rebecca had her own room with a single bed in it and her own wash basin. The window of her room overlooked the cliffs and the beach, it was a lovely view.

They were to have dinner each night for three nights in the large dining room and they had a table just for the three of them, but there were other guests on their holidays as well and the room was quite busy.

The waitresses were very smart, with white aprons over their black blouses and skirts. They all looked well, Rebecca thought, and the white linen tablecloths with matching napkins were very acceptable. She felt very special here.

The first course was soup which was served in a large blue and white bowl.

'Delicious,' she remarked. 'This soup is as good as Grandma Catlow makes!'

'Do not put the whole soup spoon in your mouth, Rebecca. You're meant to sip the soup off the edge of the spoon,' Robert Tay explained.

Ignoring the comment, she continued to drink the soup as she always had done and resented any interference from him telling her what to do.

The hit across the head came from nowhere. Such a shock to both Rebecca and her mum. Robert had hit her across the head. She felt the pain immediately. It came with such force and she felt dizzy.

'I won't tell you again, Rebecca. Do as I say or you'll get another one across the other side of your head. Eat properly and do as you are told!' He spoke with such venom; his face was as red as a lobster's and his temples were pulsating.

Marian tried to calm him down. The dining room went totally quiet and you could hear a pin drop. Rebecca glared at him. She didn't cry but you could see the hatred in her stare. She would not let this man see he had hurt her and she obeyed him when he sent her up to her room.

She remained in her room until breakfast time the following morning when Marian tried to console her.

'I hate him, I hate him, Mummy. He has spoilt my holiday,' Rebecca cried. 'I will never call him Daddy; he is not my daddy. Grandpa is my daddy!'

The hit across the head was forceful Rebecca reflected. *He had put some power behind it, far too much force than was necessary just for putting the whole of a soup spoon in my mouth.*

There was no mention of the incident between the two of them the following day. They kept each other at arm's length and conversation was polite. Rebecca vowed never to forget what happened. *It wouldn't happen again, she would not just sit and take it, no way, he would be made to pay for this.*

The second week of the holiday brought its own happiness for Rebecca. They saw an advertisement in the local paper for a puppy needing a good home. The puppy was about thirteen weeks old. They visited an old house which was slightly run down and there, behind the shed door in complete darkness, was a pair of large eyes looking up at her.

The puppy was adorable and the hairiest creature Rebecca had ever seen. He could be described as the original shaggy dog with a rough long-haired grey coat and appeared so intelligent.

The fuss the puppy made of all three of them was delightful. There was no question of the Tay family leaving the puppy behind. It was so sad to imagine what the puppy had gone through all alone in the darkened shed, and how happy he was now to be out in the daylight. Suffice to say, the puppy came home with the Tays.

It had never travelled in a car before and was travel sick several times on the journey home. Rebecca knew how the dog felt as she also got travel sick if she went on a long journey in the car. The blue Morris Minor, which again had been borrowed from Robert Tay's work colleague, was full to bursting when they all got in it, what with all their luggage and now the added extras of dog food and dog bowls. Rufus, as he was already named, sat with Rebecca in the back seat along with all her companions, her dolly Rosebud, and others, which she had had since she was a baby. They went everywhere with her.

Rufus, was allowed to stay the last night in Rebecca's room at the guest house before the long journey home and it was her task to walk him before bedtime. She was at her happiest with Rufus. The two of them bonded immediately. The pair walked up the clifftop road to the small car park behind the guest house. She waited for him to cock his leg a few times and then she let the soup spoon do its work along the passenger side of the blue Morris Minor. *That will sicken him*, she thought and she could hear Grandma Catlow's words in her mind…

It was Marian who saw the damage to the car as they were loading up all their belongings the following day. Robert was horrified, especially as the car didn't belong to him. But thankfully for Rebecca, they put it down to vandals, who had been heard laughing and shouting in the car park during the night. She had got away with that one! On the journey north a lot of the conversation was about the vandalism to the car and how much it was going to cost for the repair. That would be the last time Robert Tay borrowed a car from a friend.

The soup spoon incident wasn't mentioned again but Rebecca would never let it fade in her mind. She would love to get away from this man and go back to how things were before, but there didn't seem a way out; until there was the mention of which secondary school Rebecca would attend.

It was Robert's suggestion to Marian that maybe Rebecca would consider boarding school. This was explained to Rebecca in a very amicable way by Robert Tay and, to his and Marian's surprise, her face lit up. There were many, many questions to be asked to see if this would be feasible, for example, how much it would cost per term and could Marian and Robert afford the expensive school fees?

But the first hurdle was over. Rebecca seemed ecstatic with the suggestion of going away to school. She believed her prayers had been answered because it meant that she could finally get away from this controlling man. She loved her mummy and would miss her terribly, but it would be an adventure.

She perused the prospectus of the school which was across the Lancashire County border in the West Riding of Yorkshire, about two hours' drive across the Yorkshire moors from her home.

Yes, boarding school was the answer, just the thing!

CHAPTER 5

The news of boarding school wasn't gratefully received by both sets of grandparents and the rest of the family. Marian got it full force from Grandma Catlow:

'Marian, that is unthinkable, sending the child away from her home to school, that is cruel. She has already moved home and now she has to get used to another place without you. It's him, isn't it? He wants rid of her; you would never have agreed to this had it not been for him!'

Grandma Catlow was beside herself and Grandpa wasn't best pleased either. They missed the two of them enormously, but did visit them once a week on a Wednesday when they went to Marian and Robert's for their tea. If Rebecca was away, they wouldn't see her from one week to the next.

'Mum, it's Rebecca's choice. She wants to go. She's very happy to have this opportunity. Robert says he wants the best for her and thinks it will do her good. She really doesn't want to attend the local secondary school. Ask her yourself,' Marian explained.

Grandma was so upset. 'She's just got in the way, that's why he's sending her away. He doesn't want her. Anyhow, how are you going to pay for the fees? You work hard enough and will have to work even harder to pay for it all,' Grandma argued.

But the decision had been made and there was nothing

Grandpa and Grandma could do. Their only consolation was that Rebecca seemed to be happy with the arrangements. She told her grandma not to be upset, as it was for the best. She made no mention of the holiday and the hit across the head by Robert Tay. That was for another time. The sooner she got away from him, the happier she would be.

Rebecca and her parents made the long car journey to the school in an old Ford Popular, a dirty brown colour, again another borrowed car. They still couldn't afford one of their own.

The purpose of this first visit to the school was for Rebecca to sit the entrance examination and, if she passed this first hurdle, she would be accepted at Brantham Grammar Boarding School.

Her education would be partly funded by their local council for the duration. And to give Robert Tay his due, he did fight tooth and nail with his local council for this funding which he won in the end. But it was inevitable that some of the family members were very sceptical about his reasons for wanting Rebecca away at school.

Marian chose to believe it would be for Rebecca's own good. She felt, as did Robert, that Rebecca would receive a more structured life at this co-educational boarding school away from the claustrophobic life she had as an only child.

Robert knew his control on Rebecca was limited. They didn't really like each other but the two of them made good for the sake of Marian who was a wonderful wife and mother. Maybe they would get on better when Rebecca was away and that, on her home comings, she would be more amenable. Only time would tell.

She had passed the entrance examination with flying colours and the interviews with the headmaster and headmistress seemed to go well.

They accepted Rebecca in to the school and she was to start in the Autumn term, September 1962. She would be eleven years of age.

She was to live in the girls' boarding house, which was about a two-mile walk from the school, 'twixt two villages of Low and High Brantham, a very rural area surrounded by farms and moorland.

As the school term approached all was busy in the Tay household. There was a long check list of items she would require for school and these had to be ticked off as they were packed in the large, brown trunk with metal runners along the sides.

There wasn't much room in the lounge of the small house. The school trunk took over the room with her uniform and the many other items which were required. Rebecca's own blanket, needlework box, mufti clothes for evenings and weekends sat along most surfaces and chairs in the room. It was a comprehensive list as she would need the items for general living over the next few years of her education at Brantham.

It was an exciting time and Rebecca couldn't wait to wear the school uniform, especially the blazer. It was blue with gold edging and the tie and scarf were also the same with alternate stripes. She had a white shirt underneath the blue gym slip and long, grey socks.

Each term was about six to eight weeks' duration. Pupils were allowed half a day on a Sunday afternoon to either go home or to go out for tea with their parents as long as they were back by

7.30 pm on the Sunday evening, before suppertime and lights out. This special day was known as Exeat Day. How the pupils looked forward to Exeat Sunday when they could receive treats and visit friends and family away from the structured routine of school life, a most welcome break indeed.

Back at home, Rebecca remained very excited at the prospect of going to Brantham. She couldn't wait to tell her grandma and grandpa and the rest of her family what it was like on her visit. They appeared pleased for her as they didn't want to dampen her spirits. That wouldn't do. So, all enthused about the forthcoming arrangements, even though their darker feelings, as to why she was being sent away, remained private. Yes, things were certainly going to change a lot more for this close-knit extended family.

The summer holidays seemed to fly past and before long it was time for Rebecca to make the journey again, across the Yorkshire moors, to her new school. Robert borrowed a vehicle; a van, with a long seat in the front which accommodated the three of them.

She said her fond farewells to Rufus. She would miss her constant companion but would see him on Exeat Day in about three weeks' time.

There was a lot of luggage and the trunk was extremely heavy. There was no mistaking the trunk for Rebecca's as it had her name emblazoned down both sides in white paint. And the tuck box... well, that was huge, nearly as big as the trunk. Robert had had it specially made, but unfortunately it was treated with some sort of foul-smelling substance and thus made all the produce within the box stink. It took ages for the smell to disappear, therefore Rebecca had to leave the box open to let the air in and subsequently had to throw most of her tuck away. Still, it ended up being a great box when the smell left it.

The three travellers and their load arrived in the small market town of High Brantham at about teatime on the Sunday evening at the beginning of September for the start of Autumn school term. They drove into the gravel drive of Moonacre, an imposing three-storey grey granite stone house with large windows each about eight feet in height, which was situated between the two villages of High and Low Brantham.

This was to be Rebecca's home for the next few years whilst a pupil at Brantham. There were only a couple of cars parked in the driveway, no reception committee waiting to greet them. They must have been one of the first families to arrive.

The three looked like lonely figures as they entered Moonacre by the heavy oak front door which led into the porch. The inner door creaked as it closed behind them. The corridor ran to the left and right. *Which way to go was the question,* thought Robert.

The decision was made for them when they were met by a tall, elderly lady with a booming voice:

'Hello folks, welcome to Moonacre. I'm matron here. I do hope you had a good journey.' She fixed her eyes on Rebecca and virtually ignored Robert and Marian who introduced themselves to the matron, Miss Cross. 'You must be Rebecca then,' she stated, rather than asked, in the same loud voice.

Rebecca nodded at this strange, robust woman with the grey bun on the back of her head and a funny twitch about her mouth and nose. And she couldn't stop staring at her.

'You are early, Mr Tay, but you're not the first, there is another girl through there in Carr Hall, the drawing room; she's still sewing on her name tapes. Her parents left a while ago and there are the other older girls who won't be back until later this evening. Some of their parents live on the other side of the world in very far-flung places, you know. I have to stay up late into the night, awaiting them all, then of course it's school tomorrow!'

What a strange woman, Robert Tay thought to himself, *like someone out of a Dickens novel, the matron with the long, grey hair rolled into a bun.*

Her footsteps across the wooden floorboards were just as loud as her voice as she led them through to the drawing room.

'This is another new girl,' Matron announced, it was the name-tape girl she had previously mentioned. Rebecca went to sit beside her on the long settee and watched Harriet sewing on the name tapes. Harriet J. Bowen the name stated in blue letters on a white background.

'Mine are the same colour,' Rebecca said to Harriet, 'but my mum sewed mine on.'

'You're lucky then, aren't you? My mum can't sew and she didn't have time as she's been away,' Harriet replied.

Rebecca felt a bit sorry for the girl and said she would help her sew them on if she wanted her to.

However, Matron had other ideas and quickly ushered the Tays up the wide, stone steps and along a dark corridor leading to what was called the middle dormitory where Rebecca and another eleven girls were to sleep.

It was a little sparse. There were twelve single beds, six at each side of the room, all identical with cream, iron bedheads and cream counterpanes. The cotton curtains were flimsy and wouldn't keep the heat in the room in the very cold winters which could be notoriously bad on the Yorkshire moors. There were no plush carpets or rugs on the floor, covering the dark brown floorboards.

But Rebecca didn't seem worried at all; it was Marian who disliked this unforgiving place and hated the thought of having to leave Rebecca in this unwelcoming environment. *It will be a lot cheerier when I put my travelling rug over my bed*, Rebecca thought. She could see her mother was upset when it was almost time for them to leave for the journey home. Robert Tay showed no emotion. *Probably glad to see the back of me*, Rebecca thought.

Robert wanted to get home before it got too dark. That was his excuse for an early exit. She was also pleased to see the back of him. It would be absolute bliss not having to see or hear him for the next few weeks. Good riddance! She would see him soon enough in about four weeks' time on Exeat Day, if he came. She hoped it would be just her mum and maybe Rufus. She really would miss them. But now it was time to explore; the unpacking could wait.

She waved to her parents as they drove away in the borrowed van. Marian left with a heavy heart and their journey home was a quiet one. They had hardly turned out of the drive before Rebecca was back in the drawing room sitting next to Harriet. She liked her and they both laughed a lot together, especially at the old crow of a matron. She was a funny woman and was the butt of all their laughter.

They remained firm friends. Rebecca called her Harry and Harriet called her Becca. No one would break their bond... ever! Their beds were next to each other which was reassuring for both of them. They had made friends and everything was alright now as long as they were friends.

Another new girl arrived when they were in the dormitory. Her name was Bernadette Morrow and she told them she had a secret. She was a confident girl and seemed to have a lot to say for herself. She was to sleep on the other side of Rebecca. She was of slight build with prominent teeth and mousy brown, unruly hair.

As she unpacked her trunk, she told the two best friends what the secret was, showing them a very large book. Rebecca couldn't understand at first why a book of this size was a secret. *The Bumper book for Girls*, was the title across the front of it in huge red lettering. She opened the book and flicked over the first half a dozen pages. It looked like a normal book, but in the middle section, between the cut-out pages, nestled a small transistor radio, the smallest Rebecca had ever seen. It was hiding there in its secret place, where no one would find it.

Radios were not allowed, that was a strict rule. Reading in bed with torches, after lights out, was also not allowed. This girl seemed to want to break all the rules and she had only just arrived. *Wish I had thought of that*, Rebecca thought to herself. Her bright blue Perdio Piccadilly transistor radio had had to be left at home. Robert Tay saw to that.

Rebecca's radio was slightly bigger and wouldn't have fitted in a book, so it would probably have been discovered by the matron and confiscated.

Although she was undecided about this new girl, *you couldn't take away the fact that she may break a few rules and that may be fun*! Rebecca considered. She may not be the only one getting into trouble when Bernie Morrow was around. The three friends laughed together over the radio secret and promised it would remain between them, never to tell.

Chapter 6

It was exciting for the new girls to meet the older girls as they all returned to Moonacre. Each of them greeted one another like long-lost souls. They must have really missed each other whilst on their long summer holidays.

Some of the girls had skin which looked very tanned because they lived abroad in hot countries, where their parents were working. The stories they told one another about their holidays in these far and distant places seemed so exciting. It made Rebecca's holiday in Cornwall seem very tame, but she listened intently and noticed in detail everything about these older girls, how they spoke, how they looked and what they wore. They seemed so much more sophisticated than Rebecca and also so much more developed, physically.

Rebecca, Harry and Bernie didn't even possess a bra between them, let alone have anything to put inside one. Rebecca would refer to herself and her friends as 'the girls with two backs each'. They all laughed at that.

All the older girls seemed large-breasted for their age and every day Rebecca would check her chest to see if she had sprouted any.

It was a slow process but eventually the growing pains started and finally they seemed to just appear. *Yes, there they were; a pair, but still not a very big pair, not like the older girls. Still, time will tell.*

It was difficult to sleep that first night with so much going on and lots of chatting. Lights out was nine o'clock. It was now dark outside and only the moon was there to light up Moonacre and the middle dormitory. Rebecca lay in her bed with Harry to her left and Bernie to her right. She could hear Bernie listening to her transistor radio under her covers and sucking her thumb, which was most annoying.

That won't be happening every night, Rebecca thought, *I will certainly put a stop to that.* The constant beating of the music through the headphones and worst of all, the suck, suck, sucking of the thumb was becoming very annoying. *No wonder her teeth were so prominent, always sticking her thumb in her mouth!* She would have to think of a way to detach the radio from its owner without drawing attention to herself. She was sure there would be a way.

As thoughts began to manifest themselves in the darkened dormitory, she drifted off to sleep only to be awakened by the loud clanging of the first bell which was rung by the new housemistress, Miss Carter, who was also the history teacher. It was six thirty. Time for ablutions, as Matron would call it. All the girls made their way to the washroom for their routine morning ablutions; some more quickly than others, as some hadn't even heard the first bell. They still languished in bed until the second bell rang for breakfast, then they just put on their clothes and raced down the stone stairs, omitting the ablution phase of the morning. Bernie was one of them.

There were four teams in the boarding house, all headed by a senior team captain. The jobs were rotated each day. One team served the meals in the large dining room, the second team was responsible for clearing the tables and washing up after each meal, and the third team brushed up and tidied the dormitory. And this, all before the two-mile walk to the main school.

Breakfast was a good feed, either scrambled egg or bacon, or maybe kippers. There was always a variety of home-cooked food.

Rebecca was in the team with her dormitory captain, Belinda Rudd, a nice girl who seemed to like Rebecca. She was delighted as Harry was assigned to the same team. They had a rest day, so no jobs on the first day of school. All Rebecca had to do was to make sure she took her satchel containing her new books and stationery with her before she left Moonacre.

She was glad of her blazer and gabardine as the weather had turned cold and it looked like rain. Transport to and from school was strictly forbidden. All pupils must walk the two long miles in all weathers and there would be trouble if anyone saw them receiving a lift from passing motorists. There were always teachers or governors of the school driving past keeping an eye out to discipline the girls should they falter in this way.

This school rule for girl boarders came directly from the headmaster and his wife, the headmistress. They felt the early morning exercise would be character-building for the girls and it was also good exercise before they sat in the classroom environment for most of the day.

This husband-and-wife team could be quite daunting. They were like characters from a Dickens novel, both very stern-looking and their outlook, one could say, was most Victorian. The word *leeway* was never part of their vocabulary;

46

if one was caught doing things against their rules, one would be for the high jump in more ways than one. They put fear into the pupils just by their presence alone. When walking, they seemed to glide through the corridors of the school, with their black gowns floating steadily behind them, never missing a trick.

They always seemed to be on duty. Their home was a small house a few hundred yards away from the school gates, so they could be on the school premises at a moment's notice, should they be required. It's fair to say the two of them were a force to be reckoned with. Both were tall and thin, and the headmaster had a full mouth of very prominent teeth which reminded Becca of a horse that she and Harry used to see on the way to and from school.

The girls nicknamed the horse Joss, after the headmaster.

Each morning they would walk past the horse and say, 'Good morning, Joss,' and then collapse with laughter.

Peg Wright, the headmistress, was a stern, icy woman, who hardly ever smiled. She had a gaunt, thin face with very high cheek bones and thin lips, enough to put the shivers up anyone. She was more fearsome than Joss although the boy boarders would probably tell you otherwise, as he could be pretty handy with the cane if any one of them crossed the line.

School assembly started just before nine o'clock each morning. The format was identical, with each teacher wearing their university robes and threading onto the stage in a respectful line behind Joss and Peg. It was very formal, starting with the morning hymn, followed by morning prayers and a Bible reading, always read by the prefects and second-year sixth form pupils. Rebecca was relieved she had a long way to go before she would be required to do the Bible reading. Harry and Rebecca were always distracted, it was far more interesting on the other side of the assembly hall where all the boys were!

Lessons too seem to get in the way of the laughter and giggles of these two friends. Both sat next to each other in the classroom and they became inseparable. Wherever the girls were, there was always fun and laughter and this became infectious to many of their class buddies.

As I said previously, I watched Rebecca Ellershaw Tay from afar. I joined the class mid-term as I had been unwell and it had been impossible for me to start in the September. I think it was because of my illness that I lacked confidence, so therefore I never pushed myself forward. I was always more comfortable in a supporting role.

My name is Eva Brand and oh, how I wished I could be like Rebecca because she appeared to not have a care in the world. I couldn't help myself; I was drawn into their laughter. Becca and Harry were such fun, they never seemed to sit down and concentrate on their school work. Even in lessons and prep you could hear their laughter in the quietness of the prep room.

The room was silent and then there would be spluttering and gurgling sounds of suppressed laughter. *How lucky they were to have such a laugh*, I thought to myself. I was the one with her head buried in her books but always kept an ear and an eye out for them and was ready to warn them should they be seen by the housemistress, misbehaving. I thought they would appreciate this.

They seemed to like me. Maybe it was because I always had a nice remark to flatter them when they occasionally asked my opinion about their mufti clothes, which we were allowed to wear at weekends. Rebecca was lucky; she always had new clothes – made by her mother who was a seamstress – individual styles, designed by Rebecca herself and always up-to-date. The only thing Rebecca wore that wasn't made by her mother was her Beatle jumper, a black polo neck jumper, which she wore with black stretch ski pants, the height of fashion in the 1960s. Harriet also wore the same. They were like twins, dressing like models, or so I thought, probably to impress the boys at school when they visited at weekends for Saturday lunch and later, the Saturday night film.

They always had a boyfriend; I was too shy and nobody paid any attention to me. Who wants a girl who always blushes?

CHAPTER 7

It was I who idolised Rebecca, but it was Rebecca who put some of the older girls on pedestals. They taught her to jive. Carr Hall, which was the sitting room at Moonacre, was always the place to congregate in the evenings after prep and the weekends. The huge rug was pulled back and the girls would jive with each other to sounds of The Beatles' 'Please, Please Me', Bobby Vee's 'The Night Has a Thousand Eyes', and a particular favourite, Billy Fury's EP 'Play It Cool'.

There were several more pop records, all the latest recordings usually bought from the Farmers stores shop in High Brantham. The girl boarders were allowed to shop on a Saturday morning in the local village, as long as they wore their blazers or gabardines over their mufti.

Some of the girls brought their own record players from home to play all the records. I was always embarrassed when asked to get up and jive. I was clumsy and had two left feet, so much so that Rebecca started calling me 'the red girl' because of my blushing and my mop of sandy-reddish hair. I felt very uncomfortable with this and blushed even more. It was from this moment on I saw a side to Rebecca which I would rather not have and I tried my best to keep away from her and Harry, although Harry wasn't the problem.

'How are you going to dance, let alone get a partner at the school social, Eva, if you don't practise here? You won't be able to go, you know. No one will want to dance with you,' Rebecca said, cruelly. 'You are hopeless, Eva, you get on my nerves hanging around us and not joining in. Go and do some more studying like you usually do, that's what you're good at,' she continued.

I couldn't speak. I felt so upset and I started to cry, more out of frustration because I was unable to answer her back. She was right, I was hopeless. The others looked at me. No one said anything; there was only the music playing, Elvis's 'His Latest Flame'.

I was upset and went back to the dorm. It was there I was consoled by another girl who slept in the bed opposite to me. She was always crying because she was homesick. I know now how she felt, because all I wanted to do was to go home. The girl I always laughed at, had now made me cry.

I must have fallen asleep as I was awakened by the evening bell for tea. We always had our tea before the trek down to school in the early evening for the Saturday film which we watched with the boy boarders.

The films were quite old, and in black and white ranging from, *The Thirty-Nine Steps, St. Trinian's* and *For Whom the Bell Tolls.*

I felt a little better after talking to Joan Digby, the girl who slept opposite, who tried to reassure me that I wasn't useless, I just wasn't like them and nor should I try to be. Boarding school can be such a leveller.

We must have seen *The Thirty-Nine Steps* about three times during that winter term. But it broke the boredom of being in the boarding house all weekend and we all looked forward to our visits to the school on Saturday nights; especially the girls who had boyfriends who were boarders.

Everyone got a cup of tea at the interval and a toilet break. This was the time when the girls made a run for it and found their hideaways for a kiss and a cuddle with their boyfriends; usually in the prefects' room which wasn't used at the weekends. There could be a row of boys and girls along the wall all having a snog in the dark prefects' room which I might add was strictly forbidden, and anyone being caught would be punished.

It lasted but a short time before the second half of the film when everyone legged it back to the film room, arriving in dribs and drabs so as not to cause suspicion. That would be the last time they saw each other until the following morning at the church.

The boy and girl boarders took up most of the pews in the small Church of England church, all craning their necks to see where their boyfriends were sitting and sending them love notes across the pews or a sideways glance, which all told a story.

It was then after the service they made their arrangements; times and places, where to meet that afternoon on the weekend walk, which was the usual pastime on Saturday and Sunday afternoons.

Again, boys and girls were not allowed to meet up; this was forbidden. However, rules like this were meant to be broken and ignored by many pupils.

This was exciting for the girl boarders. One of the many walks was to Shaky Bridge, no points for guessing how it got its name. The bridge swayed from side to side as you walked across it to the other side of the River When.

Another meeting place for the pupils was Green Smithy, a small hamlet just outside High Brantham which had easy access for both the boys and girls.

It was here that the boarders would laugh and chat together and many a friendship was born on these weekend meetings. The older girls all seemed to have boyfriends from school and after meeting up would pair off together.

Rebecca and Harry didn't know where they disappeared to and had thought of following them. But if seen, they knew it would be trouble from the older girls and that was much worse than being caught and chastised by a teacher. There was a code of respect for the older girls and that was learned very early on if you were a boarder.

There was a boy at school who seemed to like Rebecca and gave her his attention. His name was Pete. Harriet had been the go-between and told Rebecca that Pete would like to meet her at Green Smithy the next weekend.

He was a chubby boy, two years older than Rebecca. He had seen her on the netball court scoring goals and had made enquiries as to who she was. He also was a boarder and had been at the school for three years.

She saw him smiling at her across the church one Sunday morning. She felt very embarrassed and didn't know what to do. What would she say if she met him? She had never kissed a boy before.

Harry had kissed a boy from the village where she lived, so she suggested perhaps they should practise kissing each other after lights out one night, so Becca would know what to do.

The two innocents decided that was the way forward.

It wasn't unusual for the girls to double up in each other's beds after lights out; it was just fun and nothing untoward was presumed. So, the two friends practised their kissing on each other.

'I can feel your teeth, Harry, should I be able to do that?' Rebecca whispered. 'It seems a bit strange, not like the couples you see in the films.'

'Do it gently, Rebecca, and stop moving your head backwards and forwards!'

The two burst out laughing. They were going to need a lot more practising, preferably with a boy who knew exactly what he was doing.

They wondered if Pete knew how to kiss, 'Well, you'll soon find out, Becca, if you meet him at the weekend,' Harry joked.

Pete offered Rebecca his biscuits and sweets as they talked by the tuck shop at school the following week. She felt uncomfortable and embarrassed and struggled to think of anything to talk about. She told him she liked The Beatles and how they all jived together at Moonacre, but he said he didn't like dancing and preferred a group called The Pretty Things, whom Rebecca had never heard of, so that was the end of that topic of conversation. He still seemed to like her though and wanted to meet the next Sunday afternoon at Green Smithy.

She became more interested in Pete as he kept winking at her across the assembly hall and across church at Sunday service.

The girls walked in a crocodile formation back to Moonacre after Sunday service, many lagged behind waiting for the boys to catch up. Pete caught up and arranged the time to meet that afternoon.

The housemistress was continually telling the girls to hurry along, so they didn't get much time to speak to each other.

It seemed a long walk to Green Smithy that day for Rebecca. She had butterflies in her stomach at the prospect of meeting Pete and knew she was going to be very embarrassed and in a way was dreading meeting him.

'They're coming now, Becca,' Harry shouted over to her.

Both were standing hidden behind the wall at the entrance to the farmer's field. Harry could see the boys walking up the country road just on the brow of the hill.

Becca was now having second thoughts, 'I'm off, Harry, I can't do this,' and after the uttering of the words, she took off rapidly back down the hill towards High Brantham. Harry was left with the task of explaining to Pete why she was there on her own. She wasn't best pleased with Becca as she walked back alone that afternoon to Moonacre. *How dare Rebecca leave her like that!* she thought.

It wasn't all bad though as Harry had met and had a laugh with the boys from school and later had met a group of local boys who all rode motor bikes. She had enjoyed being pillion passenger that afternoon riding up and down the road from Green Smithy and across the moors to a place called Big Stone;

especially riding with a boy called Fred, whose dad had a farm near Moonacre.

He had a Norton 650SS bike. The thrill she felt on the back of the bike was enormous; with the wind in her face and hair, she felt total freedom as she clung to Fred with her arms around his leather-clad waist.

This was a regular occurrence now for Harry. On her weekend walks, Fred and she became an item. She loved his slicked back hair which kept falling over his forehead and how he pushed it back with his fingers. His whole body was enclosed in black leather which Harry found most exciting. She was overcome with exuberance as she related the afternoon's events to Rebecca. She had told Pete that Rebecca was unwell, but he didn't believe that and wrote a letter to Rebecca the following day wanting to know why she hadn't met him.

Pete and Rebecca eventually spoke by the tuck shop at morning break the following day and he asked her again if they could meet up the next Saturday afternoon.

The first kiss from Pete came as they leant against the back of the corrugated metal barn which obscured the prying eyes of the others, who were all laughing and talking together. Rebecca wasn't allowed to come up for air as Pete kissed her slowly and gently. She responded naturally to his open mouth. It all seemed quite normal and Rebecca felt very happy about the way things were going. She was also very thankful that she and Harry had practised the art of necking.

They necked to the sounds of the roaring acceleration of the motor bike engines and a transistor radio playing songs by The

Searchers and Billy J. Kramer. It was a melting moment for Rebecca and she couldn't have been happier. She was so pleased that she could kiss properly and wouldn't be afraid again.

They emerged from behind the barn, Pete with his arm around Rebecca's shoulders. Both had very red mouths and were teased by the group of boys,

'Ah, Pete you've been 'Tayed,' they joked.

Rebecca wasn't sure about this comment, however she felt very grown up and couldn't wait until the next weekend when she could meet Pete again.

The following day was the first exeat Sunday and she was going home and Pete was going to his home near Manchester so they would both have to wait. After what seemed forever saying their goodbyes, Rebecca walked back down the hill from Green Smithy towards High Brantham. She didn't remember the walk as her head was full of Pete and his gentle kisses. She wondered if he had ever kissed anyone else the way he had kissed her.

The roar of the Norton interrupted her thoughts. Harry cocked her leg over the bike easily, like a professional. She kissed Fred goodbye and the two friends ran down the road together towards Moonacre, bursting at the seams to share the afternoon's experiences with each other.

'He's coming up home tomorrow with me,' Harry told Rebecca. 'Dad's collecting me after church and Fred's riding up to the Lakes to visit me at home in the afternoon.'

Harry's parents were very amenable, liberal people and welcomed all Harry's friends to their home, unlike Rebecca's parents who frowned on any boyfriends entering the house. Robert Tay saw to that, so she must be content to simply having boyfriends at school. He couldn't interfere with her life here.

On their arrival at Moonacre, the housemistress Miss Carter handed Rebecca a letter which had arrived in the lunch time post. It was her mother's handwriting and she keenly ripped open the envelope, eager to hear all the news from home thinking it strange to get a letter so close to Exeat Day. She ran up the stone stairs to her dormitory and flung herself down on the bed to read the special letter before tea.

Everyone was fine, including Rufus. Grandma and Grandpa were asking after her and sent their love and were looking forward to seeing her at half term. *Why half term?* she thought, she was going home tomorrow. *Had they forgotten?*

She soon learned that unfortunately her parents couldn't come for Exeat Day as Robert Tay had to work and her mother didn't drive. They were so sorry to disappoint her but there was nothing they could do and it was only a few weeks to the half term and they would really look forward to that.

It's all his fault once again, spoiling everything, this was to be a great weekend and now look what has happened she thought. She confided in Harry but didn't show too many emotions. She was stronger than that and wouldn't let anyone see her weakness.

Bernie Morrow was lying on her bed and would only have gloated if she had known the truth. Bernie was going out with her brothers for Exeat Day. They were both older than her. Her father was a surgeon and was fond of the drink so it was her brothers that seemed to take more responsibility.

So, there was nothing to be done, just to look forward to the next Saturday and seeing Pete. It would come quickly enough.

CHAPTER 8

Rebecca awoke on the Sunday morning; she was angry after reading the letter from home. She had so looked forward to seeing Grandma and Grandpa and Rufus as she had such a lot to tell them.

After church the cars all arrived to take the boarders on their Exeat Day. Some went home with their parents, some chose to go out for the day and have their tea at one of the local restaurants, all returning to the school boarding houses in the early evening.

Rebecca noted the stream of cars emerging from the school driveway and the car park of the nearby pub. There were at least three Jaguars and one big, black Bentley and other sporty cars like the Sunbeam Alpine with the soft top. Rebecca particularly liked this one and imagined herself sitting in the passenger seat and Pete driving her around with her hair flowing under her head scarf, just like in the movies.

After seeing all the beautiful cars, she felt quite relieved that her parents hadn't come to collect her, she would have been totally embarrassed if they had showed up in the dirty brown Ford Pop, or the Morris Minor they took on holiday with them. In the future she would get Robert to park well away from the school gates, so no one would see her getting into the old rust bucket. How embarrassing would that be!

Harry's dad collected Harry in his red Jaguar E-type. She waved at Rebecca as they sped past her up the country road.

Rebecca wished she could have been invited to Harry's. She would have loved to see Harry's home but would have needed written permission from her parents and it was too short notice for that. She had decided not to show anyone her emotions about her big disappointment because she was stronger than that and would look forward to seeing Harry later that evening and also Pete by the tuck shop tomorrow in the morning break.

She joined some of the other girl boarders that day and they listened to music and she practised her jiving. Home was in another country for some of the other girls so they never got an Exeat Day, unless they were invited by another pupil out for tea.

Moonacre was fairly quiet that afternoon and Rebecca joined some of the others and walked into the village. It wasn't much fun without Harry, it was always a good laugh whenever she was around.

She was still very angry and the more she thought about Robert Tay, the more she hated him. He had completely ruined her Exeat Day and now it would be another few weeks until half term before she could see her mum, Rufus and Grandpa and Grandma.

She vowed from then onwards she would be no pushover for anyone and if she wanted something badly enough, she would move hell and high water to get whatever it was.

She decided that her first task was to sort out Bernie Morrow and her annoying transistor radio. She was completely fed up with the unceasing thumping of the music and the sucking of the thumb keeping her awake half the night. She knew where the radio was kept, and so did half the dormitory by now. But she would have to pick her time carefully so as not to cause too much suspicion.

She suddenly felt much better and joined the others in the shops at High Brantham. Most shops were closed but the sweet shop and cafe were open and Rebecca spent her pocket money on a strawberry milkshake and chocolate. *Yes, the chocolate seems to make everything a lot better.*

Sunday tea at Moonacre was the usual cold, uninteresting spread, as Cook was off on a Sunday evening. Cold ham salad with radishes… *who on earth would serve radishes to teenagers!* It was followed by tinned fruit and either ice cream or Carnation milk; the most boring tea ever.

Rebecca walked about grumbling and stating she hoped Cook only took Sundays off and no other day of the week. Fortunately, she wasn't too hungry as she had filled up on chocolate and red and turquoise Sarsaparilla tablets.

She was waiting for Harry to return and to hear all about the afternoon with Fred, but in the meantime, there was something she must do.

After tea Rebecca lay on her bed waiting for 'God hour' to finish on the television. There were only a couple of the junior dorm girls running backwards and forwards and they didn't take any notice of her.

The *Bumper Book for Girls* was visible just inside the open top of Bernie's bedside locker. The earphones carelessly trailed over the outer casing of the big book leaving it open slightly. Rebecca hooked a pencil underneath the wire and slid the earphones gently over the side of the book. The book closed and the headphones fell onto the wooden floor boards next to Rebecca's bed, with ease.

Quickly she removed her grandma's trusty scissors from the bottom of her laundry bag. She cut one earplug from the wire and secreted it in her pocket along with the remaining earphones.

Surreptitiously she replaced the scissors, together with the cut earphone, before skipping back along the corridor and down to Carr Hall to watch the television.

She picked her time to place the earphones over the handle of Miss Carter's bedroom door. Satisfactory, she thought, Miss Carter would surely find them now. Her achievement was complete, she felt elated. No more annoying music stopping her from getting to sleep now.

The single earphone she had severed, would be carefully secreted happily with the scissors and her soup spoon in her personal box, which she kept away from prying eyes at the bottom of her dirty laundry bag.

It was pandemonium at eight o'clock, when all the girls returned to Moonacre after their days out.

Rebecca was waiting to hear the sound of the E-type's engine, telling her Harry was back. Fred also was outside and Harry ran across to him to say her good night. Fred had visited Harry's home and met her parents and brother and they had all had lunchtime drinks together in the party room with its smart parquet floor. Rebecca thought she might like to visit one day.

It was obvious that night Bernie did not listen to her radio as she hadn't discovered the earphones missing. She appeared very smug when she learned Rebecca had spent the day at Moonacre. She over-enthused about how wonderful it had been to go home and see all her family and how they had had a lunch time party and she had consumed Champagne; in fact, more than one glass of bubbly.

But what really annoyed Rebecca was that Harry and Bernie seemed very friendly exchanging stories of the day, and she really didn't like that; she couldn't participate. *Well, she won't be looking smug for too long when she has to admit that the earphones are hers*, Rebecca thought and was immediately comforted by her actions.

First bell sounded and Rebecca awoke with a start. She would see Pete; this was her first thought. Her team with Harry and Belinda Rudd were on dormitory duty this Monday morning.

After breakfast it was a quick sweep under the beds of the middle dormitory, prior to the long walk down to school, but something interrupted the normal flow of the pre-school morning chores.

Miss Carter, the housemistress, entered Hardy Hall where the girls were breakfasting and she had a stern look across her face. She stood by the serving hatch and rang the bell.

Silence fell across the room. The girls on the washing-up team came scuttling into Hardy Hall from the kitchen to hear what she had to say. Miss Carter, without saying a word, held up the earphones. Still silence and the girls all looked from one to another; except Rebecca whose gaze was straight ahead.

'Who owns these earphones?' Miss Carter bellowed; her words echoed around the room.

'If the owner of these does not make herself known to me you will all be gaited and everyone will stay here at Moonacre this coming weekend. No one will be allowed out and the school social will also be out of bounds, so it's up to you to take your choice.'

With that she walked out of Hardy Hall and into her quarters by the front door.

Breakfast over, Bernie legged it up the stone stairs and along the corridor to the middle dormitory, leaving the dining room full of girls finishing off their breakfast.

The Bumper Book for Girls, lay closed, still inside her bedside locker where she had left it. The radio also was in the same place nestling neatly inside the cut-out pages of the book, but no earphones.

As Harry and Becca swept the dormitory, they advised Bernie there was only one thing for her to do and that was to own up otherwise everyone would suffer. The dormitory captain, Belinda, made it quite plain to Bernie that it was she who had got everyone into this mess and only she who could get everyone out of it. She must immediately go and see Miss Carter to prevent everyone getting gated.

Miss Carter accompanied Bernie Morrow into the dormitory and retrieved the book which was concealing the transistor radio from Bernie's bedside locker. No need to say, the big book and its contents were confiscated until the end of the term and fortunately only Bernie was gaited.

Rebecca breathed a sigh of relief; she hadn't expected them all to be punished had Bernie not owned up.

'I know it's you, Rebecca, who took my earphones,' Bernie said.

Rebecca looked at her defiantly and replied dogmatically, 'Prove it Bernie, you are the one who knows it all so just prove it.'

'I'll remember this Rebecca, so just watch your back; you'll get your comeuppance one day.

That was their fate with each other sealed.

CHAPTER 9

The two friends, as usual, walked down to school together. The chat was mostly about Miss Carter finding the earphones and how they got into her possession without her finding the big book.

This was something Harry couldn't understand and it niggled at her: How come the earphones were found and not the book, with the radio in it?

Rebecca did not disclose her actions to Harry. The only comment she made was that they must have fallen on the floor and how unlucky was that.

The look on Harry's face said it all; she was beginning to dislike what she was seeing in Rebecca, especially over this Bernie incident and she couldn't understand why they were so hostile to each other. Perhaps things would sort themselves out soon and all would be back to normal. She hoped so.

It was the school social in three weeks' time and all the chat was about who was going to wear what dress and which boys they each would dance with. Harry's head was full of Fred from the farm and Rebecca's thoughts only on Pete.

There was no doubt about it, Rebecca's mind was never on her school work. She seemed to concentrate periodically but then her mind wandered and she was warned several times for gazing out of the window.

Her best subjects were English language and English literature but all other subjects bored her; she had no interest; she just went through the motions awaiting every break in order to socialise.

She enjoyed her hockey, netball and rounders and was captain of all these school teams at some stage. She enjoyed playing against other schools in these sports at weekends and was known for her leadership qualities when picking a team.

It is a pity it didn't overflow into her academic subjects.

There came a time in that first term when Harry and Becca were split up.

They caused disruptions in the classroom when sitting next to one another and it was decided that a sideways move for one of them might benefit the whole of the class. Harriet would join another class in the same year in order that the two of them might improve and concentrate more on their studies and less on each other and fooling around.

That was a blow to the both of them. They were extremely unhappy about this new move and Rebecca missed her best friend terribly. However, all was not lost because the friends could still be together on the walk back from school and at Moonacre, no one would dare to interfere with them there.

On the walk back from school that evening they called at the village bakers and gorged themselves on fancy cakes.

Rebecca didn't have much money at this time during the term; she had spent most of it at the tuck shop, but Harry's dad was a sweet, generous man and always sent Harry five pounds if she was ever short of money and that kept them supplied with cakes for the long walk home for several days.

They were always starving at the end of the school day. Neither touched the school lunches as they were ghastly, so apart from tuck shop food and goodies they made in domestic science classes they didn't eat.

Their last proper meal was a Moonacre breakfast cooked by Miss Livingstone, the resident cook. A nice, quiet lady but very thin for a cook.

Tea at Moonacre was pretty good. It had to be in order to make up for the terrible school lunches. Sometimes there would be a bowl of hot soup or thick vegetable broth all homemade by Dr Livingstone, as all the girls nicknamed her. They would joke, I *presume* you made this today, Dr Livingstone? And she would laugh and pretend to chase after them with her wooden spoon.

Miss Cross, the matron, would sometimes drop an aspirin in the soup, that's if it was a cold day and the girls were wet after their long walk home from school.

The serving team always served the food of the day and second helpings were always available if required, so the girls were never hungry. There were also piles of toast, cheese and jams on the supper trolley which was usually served after prep in the evening. It was always a scramble at teatime. The girls couldn't eat their food fast enough before asking for seconds.

That evening the girls were all deciding what to wear at the school social which was an important date in the school calendar. Rebecca wanted to look her best and had written to her mum and asked her to make a new dress for the social. She had sent Marian a rough sketch. It was to be pale blue crêpe with the skirt cut on the cross so that when Rebecca jived the skirt would swirl. It was also to have small, white, pearl buttons down the front of the bodice. Yes, Pete would find her irresistible in this new dress.

The reactions of some of the other girls said it all. Her mum had done her proud and she really did look a picture in the designer dress.

Rebecca complimented the older girls on their choice of dresses but when it came to Bernie's dress, Rebecca just laughed at her and said the dress looked cheap and was badly made. She continued to ridicule Bernie and told her she looked stupid and no one would be interested in her let alone ask her to dance.

I didn't want to go to the social at all. Joan Digby and I preferred to remain at Moonacre and watch television on the Saturday evening.

We felt uncomfortable, it just wasn't our thing and we were conscious of making fools of ourselves.

Bernie was no pushover and came back ferociously at Rebecca.

'No one will want to dance with you dressed up like a fairy on the top of a Christmas tree with your dyed brassy hair. I don't know what Pete sees in you. Why would he want you when he can have me?'

The comments hit a nerve. Rebecca lunged forward and grabbed Bernie by her long, unkempt hair. They pulled at each other's hair and in doing so travelled out of the dormitory and along the corridor to the top of the stone stairs outside the senior dormitory. All the while, they kicked and screamed at each other. It was only when the head prefect, Isobel, intervened that the fighting stopped.

The girls' hair fell out over their shoulders and clothes in clumps.

Both were exhausted and their cheeks were bright red but the hate in both these girls' eyes was astonishing. They were sent back to the dormitory and were sent to bed without supper.

In the quietness of the dormitory, Bernie's words kept going around in her head. She could hear her sucking her thumb which she did every night in order to help her sleep. She never seemed to let anything worry her and that also annoyed Rebecca.

How her head hurt the following morning! She was sure Bernie's head was just as sore and there was still lots of loose hair that came out and fell to the floor each time she brushed it.

The only punishment they were given, was that for the rest of the week they had to wash up after every meal. This was a much better chore than being gaited. They completed the washing-up punishment in silence and never uttered a word to one another.

Bernie was out on her own; she had no particular friend in the boarding house as most of the girls she befriended were day pupils and she only saw them at school. She also befriended some of the younger girl boarders who were under eleven years old. They all looked up to her because she was older, but she was no longer a part of Rebecca and Harry's group, not now anyway. They sent her to Coventry, as the saying goes, not involving her in any of their escapades and acting as if she wasn't there.

The atmosphere was quite strained especially in the dorm as

they slept next to one another, but Rebecca, with the scorpion sting in her tail, was unforgiving.

School was uneventful the following day, Rebecca was just happy to talk and laugh with Pete and his friends and there was no mention of the fight with Bernie and her comments about Pete.

There was quite a large crowd of pupils who all met at break times by the tuck shop. Mixing or pairing off with each other was against school rules so, if a member of staff happened to walk by, the boys and girls had to separate quickly but as soon as the danger was over, they were back together again.

Some days the girls all met at the lunchtime break down on the banks of the River When. It was a lovely setting and the girls nicknamed the grassy banks and bushes 'The Wilderness.'

The younger girls built dens in the bushes but Rebecca and her friends hid behind the giant fir trees having a smoke and talking about the current scandal of the day; and boys of course.

A fun pastime of Harry and Rebecca's was to swing out over the river on the overhanging branches of the trees occasionally getting very wet but always ending in fits of laughter and returning to the classroom in saturated uniforms.

Rebecca missed Harry in class but both made other friends. She always sat in class with Helena Austwick, another girl boarder who slept in the same dormitory. Some of their other friends were day girls. They arrived each day on the school bus from the surrounding villages and towns.

There were two special day girls, friends Lynn Barton and

Rose Parker, and the four girls had lots of fun and found lasting friendships. It was nice for the girl boarders to hear stories from outside school and what the day girls had been doing in the evenings.

The boarders didn't do much apart from their prep and then either dancing or watching television at Moonacre. Leaving the boarding house was strictly forbidden on school nights, so they had to make their own fun.

Rebecca's head eased, it was a lot less sore and the little lumps had gone down slightly. She and Harry walked back from school together as usual at the end of the school day saying good evening to Joss, who always came to the gate to greet them and to be stroked. Thank goodness it was the end of another week with all its drama and now, there was the school social to look forward to the following night.

Rebecca had an excited feeling in her stomach when she awoke on the Saturday morning. She even felt friendlier towards Bernie and spoke to her for the first time since their altercation, even though her words fell on deaf ears. But that didn't worry Rebecca, not this morning anyway.

After breakfast and the completion of the daily chores, including the peeling of the potatoes for Sunday lunch after church on the following day, the two friends and Helena, who fitted into the group very well, set off to the shops in the village wearing their mufti. They wore their blazers over thick sweaters as it was a cold Yorkshire morning with a mist covering the top of Ingleborough.

Rebecca had a list of what the three girls needed that day. She had put money aside to buy a Poly blonde hair bleach, as she had decided she needed a new look for the social. They laughed as Harry said she was going to go black sapphire and that they would need to both wear hats in the assembly hall on Monday morning so as to not draw Joss and Peg's attention to them, as dyeing their hair was not allowed.

Helena laughed with the girls and went off to purchase the new Hollies record.

When they had finished their shopping, it was all back to Mrs Big Nose's Cafe near the railway station for a cup of coffee and more laughs.

Mrs Big Nose, was the name they gave the lady owner, they didn't know her real name but she had the largest nose ever seen. She was kind to the girl boarders and let them hide in the rear of the cafe when Peg, the headmistress, collected her large, sliced, white loaf from the bakery.

Mrs Big Nose sometimes held funeral teas in the back as it was separated from the shop by a sliding door. They could hear Peg asking for her bread and oven bottom cakes from behind the sliding door, trying to suppress their giggles and Mrs Big Nose passing the time of day with her, knowing that the girls were hiding in the back. All in all, a good start to Saturday and there was still much more to look forward to.

It was pandemonium at Moonacre when the girls arrived back later that afternoon, all were pushing and shoving to be the first to have a bath. The fragrances of different perfume sprays lingered along the corridors. There was so much excitement, each girl trying their very best to look as good as the next. All looked lovely in their new dresses with their hair immaculately brushed into the latest styles.

Many of the girls including Rebecca wore ponytails which naturally swung from side to side as they practised their jive with each other in Carr Hall before the coach arrived to transport them down to school. This was a special evening hence being transported by coach, which was to be at Moonacre at seven o' clock.

The younger girls looked on in envy and amazement at the transformation of their older sisters and commented on how beautiful they all looked. They had a special tea that evening as they were too young to attend the social. Once you had reached eleven years you could attend, but not until then.

Rebecca's hair was now bright blonde and Harry's… very black; in fact, she had stained her fingers in the process of dying her hair and this took away a bit of the glamour as her hands looked as if they had been washed in mud.

Rebecca couldn't help collapsing in fits of laughter and this permeated around the dorm and before long all the girls were laughing at Harry's hands, including Harry.

Bernie was allowed to go to the social much to Rebecca's annoyance as she thought she would have been gaited up until half term at least.

Rebecca felt special in her new dress and in fact looked far more attractive than Bernie did in her shift dress with its dull colours, which looked cheap and just hung on her.

Rebecca's ponytail was tied up with a ribbon made of the

same blue crêpe which matched her dress, she was sure Pete would find her irresistible. She felt like the belle of the ball.

The school social was held in classrooms six and seven in the new buildings. Both rooms could be made into one. They were usually separated by a sliding concertina door.

The pupils crowded into the party room, the music was already playing and surprisingly enough, the lights were dimmed. The Searchers' latest record was playing, 'When You Walk in The Room'. *How apt*, Rebecca thought.

Pete was across the other side of the room with a crowd of boys. He looked very grown up in his Ben Sherman shirt with its button-down collar. He smiled at Rebecca as the group of girls from Moonacre walked in the room but had in his mind that he must be careful not to show too much attention to her as teaching staff were always on the lookout and would become suspicious.

The Moonacre girls took to the dance floor. They had been practising their dance routines for weeks prior to the social. Sometimes they jived, then they all danced in formation. It wasn't too long before many day girls joined in to the formation dancing, copying the boarders and their practised routine.

The boys were not great at dancing and stood back to watch, so the girls strutted their stuff in front of them.

Rebecca was too busy dancing to notice Bernie Morrow joining the group of boys on the edge of the dance floor. It was only when Pete started to dance with her that alarm bells were set off in Rebecca's head.

Belinda Rudd danced over to Rebecca, 'Look over there,

Becca,' she mimed and gesticulated in Bernie and Pete's direction.

Everyone knows that sinking feeling in the pit of your stomach; Rebecca now had that feeling but carried on dancing regardless. It was early in the evening and maybe Pete was trying to take any suspicion the staff had away from him and Rebecca.

After two dances with Bernie, he came over to Rebecca and told her to meet him in the sixth form prefects' room at the break. A slow dance before the break, she and Pete danced to Billy Fury's' Halfway to Paradise' and Rebecca felt in paradise dancing with him, so much so she forgot about Pete and Bernie dancing together.

A group of the girls walked to the washrooms during the break in the dancing, then their walk developed into a run. Those that were going to the sixth form cloakroom that is. This room was unoccupied at weekends and was the ideal place to meet Pete now the night was dark.

The room was also very dark but she could hear the whispering of the other couples who were all lined up against the wall, necking with each other.

He pushed her into the corner, a private place between the wall and a row of lockers. No one was interested in watching them as his hands went on a voyage of discovery rubbing Rebecca's back and unhooking her bra in the process. He placed his hand under her dress and bra and rubbed the protruding nipple between his thumb and finger. The sensation was incredible and she did not want him to stop. He sucked at her mouth and pushed his body up against her. The hard wall hurt the small of her back as he pushed her even harder.

They were disturbed by the other couples making their way out of the room all frantically heading back to the social before any member of staff missed them.

The sixth form room emptied as quickly as it had filled up.

It was difficult for their eyes to adjust to the undimmed lights of the party room as they re-entered, Rebecca was still reeling over what had just happened and she felt so happy; Pete must really love her!

She joined her group including Harry who was eagerly waiting until the end of the social to meet Fred at the school gates. She was to leave a little earlier so they could spend some time together under the trees whilst they waited for the coach.

Pete joined his friends but it wasn't long before Bernie seemed to have her claws in him once again. They started dancing together again, firstly to the 'Hippy Hippy Shakes' by the Swinging Blue Jeans and then the slow dance, one of Rebecca's favourites, 'Will You Love Me Tomorrow' by the Shirelles. This made Rebecca furious and all she wanted to do was cry. She knew all the words to this song and remembering what had just happened with Pete, she was deep in thought.

It seemed to her, that Pete danced with Bernie for the duration of the school social. He never once walked across the room to speak to her nor did he ask her to dance again. Bernie knew rightly that Rebecca was angry and jealous but she had a score to settle and this was her way of doing that. She would make a play for Pete and take Rebecca's boyfriend away directly under her eyes.

Rebecca couldn't see Bernie in the queue for the coach as she lingered with the other girls awaiting the coach to arrive. It was a little time before she saw Bernie running from the direction of the sixth form locker room. She was out of breath, her mouth was all red and her hair was dishevelled, but to be honest her hair always looked as if she should put a brush through it.

She gloated at Rebecca, 'Shame about you and Pete, that didn't last long, did it? I said you'd get your comeuppance; I'm meeting him tomorrow as well. You and him are finished.'

The words hit Rebecca like a hammer to her heart, Pete was all she cared about and now Bernie had taken that away. She had never felt such hatred for a person before.

That night privately in bed she cried herself to sleep but not before she remembered Grandma Catlow's words, 'What goes around, comes around, Rebecca.'

CHAPTER 10

Rebecca was pleased half term had arrived she would now look forward to going home and put the angst behind her.

She had decided not to dwell on the Pete-Bernie saga and behaved as nothing was worrying her. She even adopted this stance with Harry; that the incident no longer bothered her in the slightest.

Parents and the like arrived at the school gates to collect the pupils.

There was a queue of traffic, just the same as a taxi rank; car doors slamming and shouts of 'Goodbye, have a great holiday', were heard amongst the revving car engines as they drove away with hands waving out of the windows,

'Bye Harry, see you next week,' Rebecca shouted as Harry and her brother left, all excitedly waving to one another.

Half term was nine days' holiday and Rebecca was pleased to be going home. Her ride home was with another girl and her parents who lived in the same area. She was relieved Robert hadn't come to collect her; she couldn't be doing with him right at this moment in time.

Rufus went mad when he saw her. He was so excited, like a whirling dervish, repeatedly circling the room with excitement. Marian also seemed happy. She had missed her daughter over these last few weeks and felt desperately upset having to tell

Rebecca that she and Robert couldn't collect her on Exeat Day. She just hoped this half-term holiday would pass off amicably between the two of them. Maybe they would both now have had time to reflect and accept each other, but only time would tell.

Family friends arrived at the Tay household the day after Rebecca arrived home from school: Auntie Peggy and Uncle Bill with their son Andrew who was two years older than Rebecca. They had grown up together as Marian and Peggy were firm school friends and it was wonderful to see them and catch up with 'Drew' as he was generally known.

It was Drew's birthday in a few days' time and he was having a party at his house on the Saturday night and Rebecca was invited. Bill and Peggy were away for the weekend so it was to be a small party with just a few of Drew's grammar school friends. Rebecca could stay overnight and return home the following day.

Marian thought that might be a good idea, happily knowing Drew, who was a sensible young man, and very trustworthy, so she allowed Rebecca to attend the party. Needless to say, Robert Tay disagreed with his wife and rebuffed Marian in Peggy and Bill's presence, which left a bad feeling between them all.

Drew explained to Rebecca, that he and his friends were mods and it was going to be a mod party with all the music playing that mods liked to dance to.

'That's okay, Drew, I'm a mod as well,' she replied, not knowing really what a mod was. She had heard the term being used 'mods and rockers' and knew she wasn't a rocker, so therefore thought she must be a mod.

An overnight vanity case was packed and on the Saturday morning she left the house when Robert was away at work. She caught the bus across town to Drew's house which was a lovely, large detached house set in its own grounds sporting a good-sized garden pond.

Rebecca was given her own bedroom which was decorated in a chintz style with matching curtains and wallpaper, something she had never seen before. There was also an old loom-type basket chair painted in a bright pink colour and the cushions also matched the curtains. *How lovely*! Rebecca thought and she decided that one day she would also have a room like this and it would all be her very own.

There was party food to help prepare and Rebecca busied herself, helping Drew and a few friends he had been commandeered to lay out the party spread. There was also a drinks bar to set up in the kitchen area, thought to be the best place for drinks.

Rebecca wore the new dress she had worn at the school social and very lovely she looked. Drew's friends were all older and they had short cropped hair with short fringes; both the boys and the girls. Rebecca didn't feel out of place, she felt part of the crowd and everyone was very friendly and pleased to meet Drew's cousin.

It was a great party and she learnt how to dance the mod way to the Tamla Motown and soul music. Some were obscure sounds she had never heard before; her favourite was 'Washed Ashore' by The Platters and 'Going to a Go-Go' by Smokey Robinson and The Miracles. If she wasn't a mod before, by the time the party was over, she had certainly been converted.

Lambrettas and Vespa scooters crammed the driveway; this was the mode of transport for mod boys. Scooters for mods and motorbikes for rockers. *I suppose Fred must be a rocker as he rode a Norton 650SS,* Rebecca thought,

The alcohol flowed freely; vodka and lime was Rebecca's favourite although it was meant to be an alcohol-free zone.

Crowds poured through the front door; she didn't realise Drew had so many friends. He eventually told her he hardly knew any of them and also said that, once word got out there was to be a mod party, it had travelled so fast amongst the 'in-crowd' as they were known, that everyone who was a mod had turned up at the party.

How great is that! I will be able to gatecrash other mod parties, now I'm a mod, Rebecca thought.

She fell into bed about five in the morning her head spinning and the room constantly appearing on its axis. She managed to take herself off to the bathroom where she was violently sick, vomiting at least four times between five o'clock and ten o'clock that morning. All she felt like doing was sleeping, but she knew she had to go home at some stage that morning.

Her mum had been phoning the house, but to no avail; there were comatose bodies lying everywhere and no one picked up the telephone.

Eventually, looking rather the worse for wear, Rebecca arrived home in the middle of the afternoon. *What a great party it was, she couldn't wait to tell her school-friends she was now a mod, she would dress, walk and dance now just like the mods do.*

However, her happiness was short-lived as Sunday afternoon brought its own sadness. Rebecca could tell her mum had been crying when she arrived home. She was clutching tightly in her hand a newspaper advertisement showing a small house for sale near to where grandma and grandpa lived and she soon learned her mother and Robert had disagreed over the party and it had caused great trouble between them, leaving her mother distraught.

Anger welled up in Rebecca's veins. *How dare he treat my mum like this!* she thought. *Who does he think he is to upset my mum this way?*

As she was thinking this, he stormed into the front room where Rebecca and her mum sat and demanded to know where she had been and what she had been doing all night and all that day.

She couldn't speak as he ranted and raved at the both of them; Marian for agreeing to let her attend the party and Rebecca for being late home. The bedlam agitated Rufus, who anxiously barked and growled at Robert so much so that he kicked out at the dog and threw the small wooden stool in his direction hitting Rufus across his back and causing him to whimper.

Robert then landed a heavy smack across the side of Rebecca's head, dealt with gusto as only he could do. He picked up the dog chain and whipped her with it across her back. She could feel the heaviness of the chain through her leather coat and the thick Sloppy Joe jumper she was still wearing. It was unimaginable to believe he was slashing at her, with Rufus's dog chain lead. She could feel the stinging across her back, the chain leaving a long, red weal about eight inches in length in the middle of her back.

After recovering from the blow, she stood next to her mother, placed her arms around her mother's neck and jumped up, kicking Robert Tay in his stomach and legs. She was screaming at Robert and her mother was crying, which hurt Rebecca more than any physical violence he had inflicted on her.

Why had it all come to this? Rebecca thought, it was devastating see her mother carrying such anguish and she knew it was time for her to leave the house, even though this was against her mother's wishes. She could no longer live with this monster and she wondered how her mother had put up with it for so long. There was no reasoning with him; what he said to her mother had to be obeyed and he expected Rebecca to be the same condescending character.

Marian was a quiet lady and wanted a quiet life but her daughter was not a chip off that block and would not be pushed around.

It was time for her to leave.

Once again, she packed her vanity case along with an old hold-all and set off to the bus stop. She was going to where she belonged with Grandma and Grandpa; kind, gentle people who loved her and where she was always at her happiest. Back to her old bedroom with the Victorian bed and eiderdown and the airing cupboard which made comforting sounds when the tank was filling up with hot water.

She would spend the rest of her half term with them and maybe Rufus and Mum would visit her. She didn't want to lay eyes on Robert Tay; not for a while anyway.

Barbon Street hadn't changed one little bit. Everything was the same except for a new hearth rug. Grandma had sent Grandpa off into town to buy a new rug for the living room, with strict instructions that it must not be blue nor have any blue in it.

Rebecca chuckled to herself, as Grandma explained how Grandpa came home with the rug, which was predominantly blue and he'd only realised, when he was on the bus home, that the border was blue.

'Damn and blast,' grandpa said to himself. 'How am I going to get round this?'

The said rug however lay in front of the roaring fire, as if it had always been there and the blue colour didn't look too bad, although Rebecca was sure Grandma would have given him what for!

With open arms Grandma and Grandpa welcomed Rebecca back.

They were horrified to hear what had gone on earlier in the day and also about the other incident with the soup spoon, when on holiday in Cornwall.

'You will stay here young lady until such time as you are due back at school away from that man. He will not lift his hands to you again Rebecca, over my dead body,' Grandma Catlow spoke with anger.

After a few days the dust seem to settle and it was time to make preparations to return to Brantham. The atmosphere in the Tay household when Grandma and Grandpa arrived, accompanied by Rebecca, could have been cut with a knife. The adults had a talk, Rebecca knew that. She was not present but knew her side would be fully supported by her grandparents.

She remained at home for the next couple of days until all three of them made the journey back over the moors to start the second part of the school term. It was a relief to get back and her parents didn't hang around for long; in fact, Robert Tay never alighted from the Ford Pop, much to Rebecca's delight.

After final goodbyes between Rebecca and her mother, her parents set off back home, Marian once again, with a heavy heart.

CHAPTER 11

Back at school with Harry, Rebecca was delighted. Harry had told her all about the school holidays; Fred had travelled up from Brantham and stayed a couple of nights in the snug on the futon, and they had spent their days hanging out at the coffee bar in the village, listening to the jukebox with its eclectic sounds of the '50s and '60s.

'Leader of the Pack' by The Shangri-Las and 'Terry' by Twinkle were constantly played; the songs telling the stories of bikers who had met their demise and their untimely deaths riding their beloved machines, leaving their girlfriends behind grieving.

The records were banned from being played back at Moonacre because one girl pupil had lost her brother in a motorbike accident.

Rebecca was very impressed by Harry's account of half term and it was decided then and there that Rebecca would go to Harry's house on the next exeat day. Perhaps she would also ride pillion on the bikes; although she explained to Harry, she was now a mod and was going to have her hair cropped so she could really be recognised as a mod.

The Monday morning after a school holiday was always the worst time as it meant adjusting again to school rules and regulations. School assembly as usual started the new week off, but to be singled out in front of the whole school, this the two friends did not anticipate and they didn't like it one little bit. What for? Why had they to go to the headmistress's room? They searched their brains, but just couldn't think of anything they had done wrong.

Together, they waited in the dark, narrow corridor in the old part of the school building outside Peg's large office, which had a view of the long school drive over the lawn tennis courts.

Stoney-faced, she chastised them unforgivably over their choice of hair colour and told them such appearances would not be tolerated.

'You look like common girls and common girls are not allowed in this school.'

Harry's black sapphire back-combed hair was piled majestically on the top of her head and the bright blonde of Rebecca's hair showed it had been bleached and was nearly white. Harry was told to go immediately and wash the dye out; Rebecca told the headmistress she would soon get her hair cut very short so most of the bleach would then be cut out. Fortunately for them they escaped further punishment and left Peg's office holding back their hysteria. At least their first day back was a good giggle in the end.

Harry missed Fred but was soon making arrangements over the garden wall surrounding Moonacre that same evening for their next clandestine meeting.

Rebecca saw Bernie and Pete that day talking by the tuck shop but she now felt reconciled to the situation; lots of things had happened since the school social and it didn't hurt her

anymore. She had other fish to fry and was going to be introduced to Fred's friend Tony. He was very good-looking; she
had seen him in Mrs Big Nose's Cafe and they had had a few
laughs over coffee. She didn't know when they were going to
see each other but she hoped it was soon.

The senior dormitory was out of bounds to the younger girl
boarders so it was always a topic of interest when the older girls
congregated and talked quietly together in a huddle. Even a
couple of middle dorm girls went to the meetings but they
were older than Harry and Rebecca. One of them was Belinda,
the dorm captain, and her two friends Pippa Jones and Penny
Hodge.

They returned all secretive, which of course incited inquisi-
tiveness from Rebecca, Harry and also Bernie, who still spoke
to Harry on occasions. Still in the dark, over the meeting, they
settled down and dormitory lights were turned out by Matron.

It must have been in the early hours of the morning, as the
moonlight danced between the trees casting shadows into the
dormitory through the thin curtains, when Rebecca was awakened by someone whispering then quiet footsteps passing hers
and Bernie's bed. Three shadowy figures passed by and disappeared up the three steps which led into the junior dormitory.
They were then followed by another two figures and from what
Rebecca could make out all appeared to be fully clothed. She
saw nothing further just heard the sounds of 'Ssh…' and then
the sound of the dormitory sash window being opened; it was
a heavy wooden-framed window and made a noise when it
was pushed upwards.

She could see three of the beds in her dormitory were empty.

Belinda, Pippa and Penny had all climbed out of the junior dormitory window, onto the kitchen roof and slid down into the back yard; they were all away. *What an adventure* Rebecca thought. She wondered where they were going and if they were meeting anyone. *Let's hope they all made it back before the morning, maybe they would take her with them next time.*

Rebecca slept a deep sleep after the first day back at school. She was now relaxed, away from the troubles at home, although she thought about her mum and Rufus and hoped they would be alright. She also remembered she must have a letter from her mum giving Matron permission to allow her to spend an exeat day with Harry and her family in the Lake District. She did not want to go home so soon after the fight with Robert and encounter more trouble.

So, when she received the letter in the post later that week, she felt a whole lot better and looked forward to going home with Harry and her brother.

She never heard the midnight wanderers returning to their beds; they were all tucked up as per normal when the first bell rang that morning, so no harm done.

How dreary; their team was on washing-up duty for the next two days but maybe she would get an opportunity to speak with Belinda and ask her where she went during the night and ask if she had met anyone.

'I saw you going out Belinda,' Rebecca said quietly, as both girls stood side by side at the kitchen sinks.

'You saw nothing Becca, alright?' Belinda replied sharply, not even lifting her head up from the sink, but Rebecca noticed she scrubbed the dirty egg pan even harder when confronted by the question.

'Look, just tell me, I can keep a secret, I won't spill the beans.'

'Just keep your mouth shut, Rebecca. Nosey got shot and busybody buried him; just remember that,' Belinda replied.

'I want to go out next time you're going, just take me with you,' Rebecca pushed.

'Don't go on Rebecca, I'll see what happens, you're too young yet and you'll have to wait because I don't know when we're going again.'

With that answer Rebecca kept quiet. She had decided she would be going out either with or without them.

On the way to school that morning she told Harry of her plea and swore Harry to secrecy. Harry had slept through it all and wished Rebecca had wakened her. *Maybe in the future she could meet Fred*, she thought.

That was a much better idea, going out into the moonlit night instead of having midnight feasts with the younger girls.

The midnight feasts were fun though, they slid slices of bread onto their knees at supper time and wrapped them up in a napkin, along with butter, jam, and cream cheese triangles ready for their feast. They toasted the bread on the end of a knitting needle against the electric fire which was fixed high on the dormitory wall. It is a wonder the smoke from the burnt toast didn't set off the fire alarm and the smell didn't reach Matron's room.

This was great fun at first, all planning to wake each other up at midnight for the feast but now there was another more grown-up challenge; it was time for Rebecca and Harry to get in on the action of midnight trips.

Rebecca couldn't wait for this new-found freedom to come her way.

Harry had arranged to meet Fred that Saturday afternoon at their usual meeting place near the River When. He would park his motor bike and they would walk off hand in hand along the river bank. Sometimes, they had a picnic at Shaky Bridge with all the sandwiches, buns and cakes bought from Mrs Big Nose's bakery. Rebecca sometimes joined them, but generally took herself off for a short while, so they could be on their own. This Saturday though was different. Tony Sands, Fred's biker friend, was with him and that pushed the two of them together.

They all strolled along the river bank, it was a fine but a crisp, cold day. They were all well wrapped up. Rebecca had the same butterflies in her tummy as she had when she was going to meet Pete. Tony was older and he had a job so she was a little scared that he would think her unsophisticated.

He had long, black hair and piercing blue eyes, which seemed to follow Rebecca all the time. He held her stare and this gave Rebecca exciting emotions, once again. He dressed in black leathers and wore heavy, black boots, proper motorcycle attire, but hardly the right attire for a walk in the country. However, Rebecca was smitten and they held hands as they walked along whilst he was constantly telling her jokes which made everyone laugh.

She soon was relaxed and enjoying Tony's company so much so she was dreading the time when they had to return to

Moonacre. They all ate the sandwiches and joined in a light beer which the boys had brought along in the panniers of their bikes. In fact, Rebecca felt a little tipsy but it was a good feeling. Afterwards, Harry and she both chewed gum, to rid the smell of the beer.

The two girls later climbed onto the pillion seat of the bikes and sped off at great speed. Rebecca couldn't believe the excitement the ride instilled in her; the wind in her face and the force against her body as she clung on to Tony's leather jacket. She leant her head against his back feeling totally protected by him as they went in the direction of Moonacre.

They stopped their bikes in the lane behind Moonacre's high wall. Tony secured his bike on its stand then grabbed hold of Rebecca pushing her up against the high wall. His lips sought her mouth, prising her lips apart and forcing his tongue into her open mouth. His kiss was ferocious, his tongue exploring every part of her mouth. She responded naturally; she had never had a kiss like this before. She couldn't move as the weight of his body pushed her up against the stone wall. She felt totally domineered and was happy to be so.

The quietness was disturbed by Harry.

'Come on you two, we'll have to get back. We'll see you both tomorrow after church. Same place, same time.'

With that the girls said their goodbyes and climbed the stile over the wall and ran across the hard tennis courts towards the back entrance of Moonacre. Rebecca couldn't wait to talk to Harry about Tony.

'He really likes you Rebecca, he's been asking Fred to arrange this day for ages.'

'I love being on the back of the bike, Harry, and can't wait until tomorrow. He's a great kisser, I hope he thinks I am as well. Maybe we can go out one night this week and meet them both.'

Harry thought that was an excellent idea and the plan was created carefully. No one must know. It was their secret.

It seemed a long evening as there was no film to watch down at school that night but the girls were not concerned as the new plan was foremost in their minds. They would arrange the meeting the next day when they met the two boys.

Rebecca was swithering, she felt like a mod, but she now had a rocker boyfriend with a great motorbike so she decided to wait a while before she had all her hair cut off. In any case Tony said he liked her long hair and she loved it when he had pulled her head back by her ponytail when he had kissed her. She liked that very much.

They watched the Saturday film on the television and then had supper before it was time for lights out. She noticed there was another meeting in the senior dormitory when all the girls were huddled round each other whispering. She knew by now what they had on their agenda, but they didn't know about hers and Harry's plan.

Once again, Rebecca was wakened, this time by the sound of the junior dormitory window being slid open. She must remember to rub some Vaseline on the sash part to stop it making a noise before she and Harry needed to use it. The night was very dark, no moonlight to lead the way for the midnight trippers this time. She knew who the girls were and they all had boyfriends; one was from the village; the others had their boyfriends down at school. They were also boarders.

Rebecca contented herself knowing she would be going out in the middle of the night very soon to see Tony. She couldn't wait to have the freedom and with that, sleep took over.

Church over, the girl boarders dressed in their Sunday best grey suits with their blue bowler style hats, badge on the front, walked as per usual in crocodile formation, back up the hill from school to Moonacre; a journey of about two miles.

Sunday lunch at Moonacre was always a good feed with a roast of either beef, chicken, lamb, or pork and all the trimmings including roast potatoes in abundance which the serving team had to peel on the Saturday lunchtime before, so there was always plenty. This was generally followed by one of Miss Livingstone's sponge puddings, usually lemon or spotted dick, with custard.

Full up to the brim, it was time for the boarder girls to go on their afternoon weekend walks in the countryside. This was traditional.

Harry and Rebecca, with the boys, were riding over to Morecambe Bay about twenty miles away. They both hoped the housemistresses were not doing their sporadic walk checks, which they did periodically, otherwise they would be in trouble. Each girl wrote down in the walk book where she was going, so she could be found if necessary. Shaky Bridge was always good, as it was not by the roadside and inaccessible by car. The housemistresses would have to walk to it and the girls could be anywhere. Yes, it was good. So Shaky Bridge was written down in the walk book and off they went to meet the boys in High Brantham as they had the day before.

Rebecca had worn her warm walking trousers, boots, with a thick Arran sweater and her three-quarter length navy blue leather coat over the top of it. The coat was new, bought for her by grandma and grandpa during the half term holiday. She felt very trendy, as the model, Twiggy, and the singer, Lulu, also wore one of a similar design.

She was glad of the layers, as she and Tony sped along the country roads which twisted and turned. She was becoming accomplished riding around the bends and did as she was instructed to do, leaning her body into the bends; to the left for a left-hand bend and right for a right-hand bend.

The crash helmet was a little too big and it kept slipping down over her eyes; in fact, it was very uncomfortable. The journey didn't take too long once they reached the M6 motorway. Tony could really open the bike up and so he did. Rebecca had never known speed like this.

All arrived at Morecambe Bay in one piece and felt exhilarated by the ride. They walked along the seafront, the boys ate fish and chips from newspaper and Tony bought Rebecca some Morecambe rock. They meandered in and out of the amusement arcades, all playing the penny ball machines, but not winning very much. They laughed a lot; it was such a lovely day.

The fairground was also open and the lure of the tattooist was just too much. On each of their forearms they had their names tattooed: 'Becca' and 'Harry' they read, never giving the consequences a thought. It was only afterwards Rebecca thought about what her mum would say. She had already warned her against ever having a tattoo.

'You will always have it and when you wear an evening dress your tattoo will show and what a common girl you will look.'

Her mum's words were forgotten through all the excitement, but came back to haunt her as the tattoo became painful and extremely red. Harry's was the same and both had to keep bathing it in antiseptic to stop any infection. It was too late now to worry about what her mum might say and it was not going to spoil the rest of the afternoon.

The four spent their time at the fair ground on the ghost train, where Tony stole a long kiss in the dark and then on the big dipper and cat and mouse. All the rides were exciting and all in all it was a brilliant afternoon.

It was almost dark by the time they arrived back at Moonacre for tea.

They were late but managed to climb in through the general-purpose room window which was on the ground floor. They hung their coats up and sauntered into the lounge where the telly was on whilst at the other end, the record player was also blasting out. The competition between the two was deafening. No one had noticed their lateness and all was normal as the bell rang for the girls Sunday tea.

Both girls wore long-sleeved jumpers, hiding the new addition to their forearms, hoping none of the teaching staff or Matron would notice.

They kept their trip to Morecambe a secret, so as not to spoil any future trips on the bikes.

But the talk that night was not about them but talk from the older girls that Matron's intention was to be present when the middle dormitory girls were taking their baths. She had always helped bathe the younger girls but to adopt this way with the girls aged thirteen years and over was just not acceptable. The girls were in uproar, including Harry and Rebecca as they thought of their tattoos. They must avoid baths in Matron's presence at all costs and went to hide in the attic when it was their allocated bath time.

The list was pinned to the notice board so each girl knew in advance the schedule of her bath time; with thirty girls in residence these times must be staggered. There were several girls who fled up the steps to the attic when Matron shouted 'Ablutions' and it became a very difficult task for Matron to police, as the older girls flatly refused and locked the bathroom door before she entered, so this arrangement fell by the wayside. The girls could breathe again and when wearing short-sleeved gym tops they covered their tattoos with a sticking plaster.

The following week Rebecca was chosen to play hockey for the school's 2nd X1, much to her delight. She was the youngest in the team and loved all sports. She was to play out on the left wing and this became her permanent position.

Each Saturday morning during the winter term Brantham Grammar School would play hockey and netball matches with schools in the area and some further afield. She was also playing for the school netball team in the goal attack position and eventually captained the team.

Most Saturday mornings there was either a hockey or a netball match, home or away, so this took up her Saturday, but she still managed to meet up with Tony in the afternoons each weekend and their relationship seemed to grow.

She missed him during the week as girl pupils were not allowed the freedom to go to the village, as this time was for prep and lights out was nine o'clock, so not much time to do anything else. She hoped Tony didn't have other girlfriends from the village as they would be able to meet him whenever he wanted them to.

Harry was hilarious though; it was a comfort for her as she could see Fred working on his dad's farm. This she did, standing on her bed dressed in her babydoll pyjamas, looking through her dad's binoculars, giving the girls a running commentary on his movements. Then, just before lights out, he would race past Moonacre revving the bike engine. This was their way of saying goodnight to each other.

The two friends, however, had arranged for their midnight adventure.

It was to be the Thursday night before exeat day Both were extremely excited because they were meeting the boys on the lane side of the high stone wall and their destination was the hay barn on Fred's farm; not too far away to walk in pitch darkness.

Both were too excited to sleep and were waiting for Fred's signal from the farm to set off. He was to flash his torch three times and then the girls would get into their outdoor clothes, which had been in their beds ready for the getaway.

Margie, who slept by the junior dormitory window, was told to expect to be awakened but she was used to this and felt as though she was trusted by the older girls so was always pleased to help.

They whispered to each other as they silently crept past Belinda Rudd's bed and up the three steps into the junior dormitory, both as quiet as church mice.

Although this was the winter term, the night was fine and they had dressed in warm dark clothing so as to be able to move without being seen. They climbed over Margie's bed and lifted up the heavy sash window. Luckily the grease had done the trick and it went up with ease.

Out they went onto the sloping kitchen roof and dropped down into the back yard by the kitchen door. Then it was away across the grounds and over the stone wall. It was an exhilarating feeling. They were so excited and nervous knowing, if missed, they would definitely risk being expelled from school, make no mistake. But they had done the hard part and wanted now to reap the rewards and enjoy the freedom for the next few hours.

The bikes were silent in the lane and all four walked up the grassy lane and across the field to the hay barn. The smell of the night was particularly noticeable to Rebecca, it smelt earthy and musty but she liked it and the smell of the hay barn seemed stronger at night. It was very dark but Fred had his torch. It was difficult to see anything when they entered the barn but soon their eyes became accustomed to the blackness and the hay bales stacked majestically towering above them but leaving a square recess for the two couples to lie down cosily using only hay bales to separate them.

They snuggled into each other; Rebecca had never felt closeness like this before. She should have been shivering on such a cold night but she felt on fire. He kissed as if he was going to eat her as he laid on top, pinning her down making her unable to move. The weight of his body was exciting and she didn't want to move. His tongue explored her mouth fervently for a time and then he became more gentle as his hands rubbed her back underneath her Arran sweater and shirt. She had left her bra off as it had been too difficult to put on under the bedcovers in the darkness of the dormitory. The Arran sweater was discarded as he sought her breasts, rubbing the nipples between his thumb and fingers. He tenderly kissed her neck and shoulders before encompassing each nipple in turn with his large mouth and sucking hard, biting the nipple with his front teeth. Rebecca lay and enjoyed the amazing feeling this caressing brought to her. Tony was the one for her and she had no inclination to stop him doing whatever he wanted. She wondered what was happening to her as she cried out.

'Ssh… Rebecca, you'll disturb the cows,' Tony whispered with his finger over her mouth. He was laughing and he tickled her. He wanted to go further but resisted the urge as he wanted to leave her wanting more. There was always this coming Sunday, exeat day, when they were to spend more time together at Harry's house.

They must have been in the barn for a good couple of hours, when all four made their way back down the lane to where the bikes were parked and the girls said their goodbyes, dreading the climb back up the kitchen roof and in through the window.

It was still very dark at half past four in the morning, when they climbed through the junior dormitory window. All around had an eerie silence and the smell of the morning mist still lingered in Rebecca's nostrils. She felt tired now but thought she would be too excited to sleep. The night wanderings were playing over and over in her mind and the feelings she had encountered with Tony were just amazing. She couldn't wait to compare notes with Harry, but that would have to wait until tomorrow.

Eventually, she slept until disturbed by the first bell, rung today by Matron, whose heavy black brogues clattered up the corridor.

She didn't need to ring the bell; the clatter of her shoes awoke everyone anyway.

The two girls didn't get out of bed straight away as they were still dressed in their jeans and jumpers so they hurriedly stripped off under the covers and made their way to the wash-rooms before breakfast.

All seemed perfectly normal; they had not been missed, not even by the other girls in the dormitory. Both were extremely tired but were pleased everything had gone smoothly and looked forward to talking about every small detail with each other.

This was done on the way down to school and Rebecca held nothing back. In fact, this was the topic of conversation all day; at break and lunch times and Rebecca herself daydreamed throughout all the lessons that day. She was extremely quiet and one or two of her classmates remarked so.

Harry had made arrangements for the coming Sunday, exeat day, which included Rebecca and Tony. They were to meet the boys at the coffee shop in the next village and then spend the afternoon riding the bikes and later having tea at Harry's house overlooking the sea.

Sunday couldn't come quickly enough, but she had plenty to occupy herself, what with hockey practice during games and the forthcoming game the coming Saturday morning.

They happily won their away match and Rebecca scored her first goal for the team against the grammar school in Settle. She took the short corner, pushing the ball straight onto the centre forward's stick, who in turn pushed it back to Rebecca who flicked it between the goal posts.

The only goal of the match and the whole team were on a high as the bus journeyed back to Brantham school and lunch at school.

CHAPTER 12

The girls had arranged to meet Tony and Fred on the Sunday afternoon in the cafe with the juke box, near to Harry's house.

Mr Bowen, Harry's dad, had collected them and Harry's brother in his black Daimler car after the church service. Rebecca wasn't ashamed of this car and wished everyone could see her getting into it. They lingered outside the church and chatted with their friends and parents alike until they all left speedily for Sunday lunch at Harry's. It was a special Sunday lunch at a hotel which overlooked the estuary to Grange-over-Sands.

The white linen tablecloths, napkins and the crystal-clear wine glasses reflected the shards of light entering the dining room, putting on a display, it appeared, just for them. How different this was for Rebecca, to be actually taken out to a posh hotel restaurant for her Sunday lunch.

Rebecca opted for the Sunday carvery. She had never had three different meats on her plate all at the same time, ever before. Pork, chicken, and beef accompanied by Yorkshire pudding, stuffing, roast and mash potatoes and vegetables. The large platter in front of her was full. It looked like she was going to climb her lunch, not eat it. She had started with a delicious platter of smoked salmon and capers, specially smoked in the hotel's smokery, and dessert was from the trolley displaying delicious mouth-watering fare, making it so difficult to make the right choice. There was also a large selection of local cheeses also beautifully displayed with celery sticks towering from a crystal jug which also caught the sunlight.

Both girls were allowed a fine, crisp glass of Chardonnay wine to accompany their meal, which went down very well indeed, but after that they were told it was water. It was such fun all chinking their wine glasses and saying cheers and Harry's dad telling stories about his boarding school days.

Harry's mother was a very attractive lady with her hair piled up on the top of her head and long, elegant, red finger nails, which were prominent as she held her cigarette holder to her mouth and drew the smoke in delicately between her lips. She was also fun and Rebecca couldn't remember laughing so much and having such a fun day for a very long time.

Feeling full up to the top after their superb lunch the girls made their way to the coffee bar. In fact, Rebecca felt a bit tipsy and couldn't stop giggling but she remembered the strict instructions that they must be back at six o'clock in order to make the journey back to school.

Rebecca couldn't even drink a cup of coffee she was so full after the sumptuous luncheon but sipped on an orange juice to quench her thirst. All her favourite records played on the juke box, 'Runaway' and 'Hats Off to Larry' by Del Shannon. Both reminded her of her visit to Harry's house and the coffee bar and in particular spending time with Tony.

Good times end too soon, she thought as she clambered back on the bike with Tony for their last spin around the Westmorland coastline, alongside the Kent estuary.

They stopped to take a motorboat trip for half an hour until the heavens opened. It looked like the bad weather was in for the rest of the day so, dripping wet through, they made back to Harry's and spent the late afternoon drying off in the party room with the boys. Life here was so liberal and Rebecca loved it. They all arranged to meet the next week in the lane next to Moonacre and go to the barn. They would wait for Fred's signal as usual before leaving the dormitory.

Rebecca felt contented on the journey back knowing she would be seeing Tony again soon and was daydreaming about the fabulous time today they all had together. The rain lashed on the car windscreen as it meandered swiftly along the country road. The window wipers were set to their full capacity. But even with this, Harry's dad found it difficult to see, his only guidance the cats' eyes in the middle of the road. After about one hour and forty minutes they arrived safely back at Moonacre, full of excitement. They couldn't wait to tell the other girls what a great day they had.

But sad to say their euphoria was short-lived.

One girl was very late returning, her family had been held up behind police vehicles and ambulances. She told of a bad accident involving a motorcyclist on a bad bend in the road. She described the black Triumph motor bike smashed up and mangled lying on the roadside next to a high stone wall. She could see no more as the ambulance pulled away sounding its two-toned horns with its blue lights flashing.

Rebecca felt a sickness in the pit of her stomach, it was agonising. Tony rode the same bike as the girl described. The feeling remained with her throughout the night, a sharp dull pain, a hurt like no other she had ever felt. There was no sleep that night, many tears but no sleep. She prayed so hard that the accident hadn't involved her beloved Tony; that was more than she could bear.

Fred met the girls on their way down to school the following morning, with the news Rebecca did not want to hear. Tony's motorbike had aquaplaned on the surface water, which was not visible in the treacherous conditions of the previous evening, along that country road. Bike and rider had skidded uncontrollably some fifty yards into the high stone wall killing him instantly.

Rebecca was stunned, her head felt light and a dagger had entered her stomach. She just wanted to fall down to the ground and her legs started to shake as she fell against Fred's body across the bike. She wanted to see Tony but didn't even know where he lived. It was as if everything she had ever cared about was lost; reality did not matter, she cared for nothing now.

Harry knew they had to get down to school so they both climbed onto the Norton with Fred and he dropped them off outside the school gates. They went straight to Matron's sick bay at school where it was explained that Rebecca's close friend had been killed in an accident on his way home and that was all. Rebecca was shaking and she felt light-headed and sickly.

Matron, a jolly lady, loved by all the boy boarders, didn't quiz Harry and Rebecca as to the relationship they had with the dead young man as she could see that both girls were visibly shaken. She decided the two would remain in the sick bay until such time as they felt ready to leave. After several cups of tea and Matron's homemade Shrewsbury biscuits, the two friends made their way to their respective classrooms.

They had missed the lunch break, so it was only a matter of a couple of hours before they could go back to Moonacre and try to find out what had really happened to poor Tony and what the funeral arrangements were.

Tony was to be buried later that week in the small cemetery overlooking the River When; a really lovely spot, but sadly Rebecca was not allowed to attend. She was overcome with grief at this ruling as she heard the words from Matron:

'The girls should not be associating with such riff-raff. He was a local lout who was killed on his silly motorbike, no doubt going far too fast. They get what they deserve.'

The words cut into Rebecca. How dare she make those disgusting observations on someone she didn't even know and she knew nothing of the circumstances. Rebecca would never forget those cruel comments and would bide her time. She reflected on the last day she had spent with Tony: firstly, the lovely Sunday luncheon with Harry and her family to the exciting afternoon at the coffee bar, the boat trip and riding pillion with Tony. She was so happy then. My, how things had changed in such a short time.

The week that followed was pretty flat and nothing to look forward to, apart from games which Rebecca loved, and matches at the weekend.

When it came to the Thursday evening, she reflected on what she and Harry had arranged to do, which was to midnight wander and meet Fred and Tony. Sadly for her, that was not going to happen, although things continued as normal for Harry.

Bernie was now in on the act and accompanied Harry in the early hours of that morning. Harry meeting Fred and Bernie meeting Pete.

She wondered if they would lie in the same place as she and Tony had lain previously in the old barn. The more she dwelled on this the more upset and angry she got.

'I hope you both get caught,' Rebecca snapped at Harry. She didn't mean those words; not to Harry anyway. She was hurt and was also jealous of the friendship Harry was having with Bernie. *Anyone else except Bernie*, Rebecca thought, *didn't Harry care at all?* She felt very let down. She must have then drifted off to sleep.

Rebecca was awakened in the early hours. At first the apparition looked like a grey ghost but she then realised it was Matron with her long grey hair falling over her shoulders and hanging lankly down her back. *A frightening sight*, Rebecca thought.

'Yes, Harriet Bowen's bed's empty as is Bernie Morrow's,' were Matron's words. Rebecca kept her head buried under her bed clothes, Matron and the housemistress at each side of her bed checking to see if her bed was also empty.

Rebecca knew they were caught; she could hear the familiar sound of the junior dormitory window sliding open. Bernie was greeted by the towering, ghostly-grey woman. Bernie, not hearing her words, turned and slid back down the kitchen roof and ran back across the fields to the barn where Harry and Fred lay.

It later transpired that Pete hadn't turned up to meet Bernie so she had made her way back to Moonacre alone. Both girls eventually returned together, but by this time the downstairs lights were blazing and Police Constable Horn was standing in the entrance hall.

Rebecca's heart was pumping so noisily she thought it would wake the whole dormitory. It was some time before the two girls returned to their beds at each side of Rebecca.

'Squealer,' Bernie savagely spat out in a whisper to Rebecca, as she climbed into bed. Rebecca ignored the remark and didn't at that time realise its significance.

The following morning Harry was very subdued. She had been crying but there was nothing Rebecca could say or do to make her feel better; it was as if Rebecca was getting the cold shoulder from her best friend and this was very hurtful.

It soon became real when she was left to walk down to school on her own. She followed on behind her best friend, who was with Bernie, but was not included in their conversation. She desperately wanted to find out what had happened from the two girls but was kept totally in the dark.

She was so sad and felt she had lost everything; first her Tony and now her best friend Harry, dear Harry's cherished friendship. It only dawned on her later that day as the cold shoulder continued, that Harry blamed her for squealing to Matron. Which did not happen!

Somehow, she would have to root out the squealer, find out who she was.

Harry looked a sad, solitary figure as she stood outside Peg's office. Her father and mother were in the headmistress's office, being told in no uncertain terms, that this behaviour from the girls would not be tolerated. They were told to remove their daughter from Brantham immediately and place her in a more suitable school nearer to their home.

And that was it. Unbeknown to Rebecca and the rest of the girls, Harry left Brantham there and then, packing all her belongings whilst the other girls were still at school. No goodbyes. It was a sad day all round. Bernie was the lucky one. Had Pete turned up she would have also been expelled. She was let off lightly with a suspension until the beginning of the next term. The end of an era, so they say.

Three more weeks until the end of the school term. Rebecca cut a lonely figure during the last few weeks, not happy at school and certainly not looking forward to the Christmas break at home. It would appear the anger and hurt were building up inside her and others gave her a wide berth. Matron's words in her head turned over and over: 'Local lout', 'They get what they deserve' and 'Yes, Harriet Bowen's bed's empty.'

It wasn't her who had squealed; she would never do that to Harry. She missed her terribly; no one to laugh and joke with and now no one to cry with. *How would she be able to explain to Harry that she had had nothing at all to do with them getting caught?*

It later transpired it was PC Horn's interrogation of Bernie who eventually admitted Harry was with a boy from the village and that is why she was expelled and Bernie treated more leniently. But it still remained a mystery who the squealer was.

However, I was quietly confident!

Rebecca met Fred in the lane at the weekend, they had much to discuss. He said he would explain to Harry when he next saw her how Bernie had broken down crying and confessed all to PC Horn.

Fred carried on seeing Harry. He loved her and it was only a short motorbike ride to see her. It was Rebecca who was going to miss her best friend and soulmate.

CHAPTER 13

I will never forgive Rebecca for locking me in the attic at Moonacre, a place which was frightening enough after hearing all the tales of the resident ghost, Boneyard. The attic was where the girls' trunks and suitcases were stored throughout the school term.

She conned me into going in there on the pretence of me helping her to get her trunk down, and like a fool I obliged. In fact, she did it because she was picking her netball team for the evening's game between the girl boarders and the day girls and she didn't want me in her team.

Every girl boarder was told about Boneyard and how he would 'get you' if you went in the attic at night time. There was many a threat by the dormitory captains that, if you carried on talking, you would be banished to the attic. Those threats silenced us all, I can tell you.

So, when the team was chosen, Rebecca made sure I wasn't available. She locked me in the wretched attic room with only one light and a small window to peer out of. Sadly, no one missed me either. That also spoke volumes. I was useless at sport and no one ever chose me for their team, especially Rebecca, because she always wanted to win. This particular day, it was only at teatime when I was missed because I was on the serving team.

The house was searched and eventually the attic door was unlocked. I had got cold and the bright light hurt my eyes, I was also hungry and thirsty as I had been locked in there for about three hours.

Rebecca's stare said it all. If I had told, I knew I would definitely be in for further abuse so I made an excuse that the door must have jammed and mentioned nothing of Rebecca leading me up there earlier that day. It was sacrilege that we never split on each other; an unwritten rule.

Although I kept shouting for assistance nobody could hear the banging and shouting over the cheering for the respective netball teams.

She was just a bully to me, but I took it because I didn't want to cause waves and draw attention to my inadequacies. Splitting on another pupil was severely frowned upon by the other girls. One has to fight one's own corner, but I found this very difficult where Rebecca Tay was concerned.

She also got it into her head it was me who told Matron about Harry and Bernie, but of course I totally denied this. That's probably the real reason she locked me in the attic, there is no doubt she suspected me.

So, I didn't get her trunk down from the attic, in fact I couldn't bring myself to converse with her at all. She didn't make me laugh anymore and I didn't want anything more to do with her.

It was nearing the end of term and the chat about end of term pranks was always to the forefront of conversations with the junior girls and it was at Rebecca's instigation that the younger boarders took up on her plan.

Tying a nylon stocking across the junior dormitory doorway to trip Matron up as she did her night rounds was the best plan they had heard.

Of course, Rebecca put herself far away from any blame, just planting the seed into the other children's minds. All giggling, it was great fun, and the junior girls put their plan in place after lights out.

They tied the nylon stocking low across the entrance to the junior dorm, from one bed leg to another, then jumped back into their beds awaiting Matron's heavy footsteps along the corridor while doing her nightly checks.

It worked a treat, her heavy shoes clattering along the corridor, through the middle dorm, up the three steps and… down she went like a ton of bricks, hitting the heavy metal trunk directly in her path. She lay over the trunk totally helpless, her legs and arms cut to smithereens. Blood escaped from the veins in her thick legs, her forehead was also bleeding profusely from a very deep gash, caused when she hit her head on the metal edge of the trunk on impact as she fell.

She was unaware of the raucous laughter that filled the junior dormitory as she lay sprawled over the trunk totally helpless. No one could help her; she was such a big woman, far too heavy to lift.

All the commotion alerted the prefects from their ground floor rooms, who were aghast at the sight of Matron, totally incapacitated on the floor, lying in a pool of her own blood.

This was serious, the prank had gone drastically wrong and soon the young girls realised their error. Matron was seriously hurt and it was their fault. They would all be for the high jump now.

In less than a week, PC Horn was back under the roof of Moonacre trying to make sense of this terrible prank which had gone very wrong. All the girls involved were under ten years therefore no criminal responsibility could be assumed, but needless to say the school would be taking some sort of action against the ring leaders.

Again, Rebecca kept her head down and felt no remorse seeing the wicked woman sprawled across the floor and the trunk, totally helpless. Grandma's words were again in her mind, 'What goes around, Rebecca…' The nylon stocking which had caused all the damage found its way into Rebecca's laundry bag!

It was to be the middle of the next term before Matron Cross returned to Moonacre. The young, coerced girls were all reprimanded. Each was given four light beatings with the slipper across their backsides with the full agreement from their parents.

The following term they were all gated and had to remain in the confines of Moonacre at weekends. All privileges were to cease until the half term anyway.

Rebecca's name was never mentioned. *Had she got with it away again?* It would appear so!

The week before the break for Christmas was always relaxed at Moonacre. The girls would do their rounds of visiting the local elderly residents in the homes in the area and sang Christmas carols to them. They were rewarded with unceasing amounts of soft drinks, sandwiches, and vol-au-vents, followed with hot mince pies and cream, all consumed in front of roaring fires. A lovely start to their Christmas holidays! The girls loved these visits and so also did the elderly residents. Then it was onto visiting the homes of the governors of the school and the doctor's home, Doctor Down, for more of the same mince pies, speciality cakes and copious amounts of mouth-watering treacle toffee, all homemade, in exchange for singing more carols.

It seemed there was always snow on the ground and the dark nights were cold, crisp, and icy, with the snow or heavy frost still clinging to the branches of the trees and the River When still frozen.

Every place they visited had their Christmas trees decorated for the occasion. Some trees were so tall and beautifully decorated with glittering baubles in all colours including silver and gold and streamers falling over each branch, some trees were even adorned with real candles which were fixed to the end of each branch and lit the trees up beautifully. Rebecca felt a warm feeling inside her; the first warmth she had felt in a long time. *I wonder how long this will last*, she thought.

Robert Tay collected the large, brown trunk from Moonacre on the last day of term and proceeded to the pub car cark, where he had been instructed by Rebecca to park the dirty brown Ford Popular car. It was his turn to do the run and collect the girls this end of term; it was the least he could do, so he thought.

Both girls ran over the bridge to the waiting vehicle and dived into the rear seats keeping their heads down until out of sight of the school. As Rebecca popped her head up at the traffic lights in the town, she was spotted by a boy boarder, a boy she had had her eye on for some time.

'Oh my God,' she shouted. 'How embarrassing is that! He's seen me.'

The boy, Eddie was his name, peered back at her from the back seat of the red Daimler, which was also waiting at the lights and he winked provocatively with a wry smile on his face. Rebecca was so embarrassed she fell across the back seat of the Ford Pop again, until she was well away from High Brantham.

'I can't believe that just happened,' she remarked, 'I am so embarrassed.'

At least Robert had a chuckle to himself, thinking that it had been worth it driving all that way in the snow.

It was the worst winter for a number of years, the snow was piled high up the telegraph poles on the way over the moors. In places it was a single-track road and still the snow was falling, piling over the roadside danger markers. Even the sheep appeared to be hibernating as they clustered together against the drystone walling with their rear ends against the driving snow.

Home at last and the house smelt of mum's homebaked deep crust potato pie, a Lancashire meal which sticks to your bones on such a cold night. The house was warm and welcoming, no wooden floorboards and draughty windows, where the draughts blew the curtains out into the room. The Christmas tree was up and positioned in the front window of the lounge, lighting up the garden, a very cosy sight.

Perhaps Christmas might be okay after all.

Chapter 14

No morning bell to waken Rebecca Tay this morning, although she awoke early to the sound of movement downstairs. Mum was probably up and around making Robert's breakfast and of course Rufus had to be walked. She only hoped *he* had already left for work. She was pleased to be home. It had been a hard term; so much to reflect on, most of it not her own doing.

She missed Harry. Things would never be the same again, losing Tony whom she was also very fond of and then the incident with Matron.

She realised this time she had got away with it. The junior girls must be protecting her by not splitting and telling all.

Yes, she had taught them well, they dared not to split on Rebecca! She decided that next term she would have to keep her head down for a while and keep the juniors happy, keep the momentum going, but no regrets, she thought. That was Matron sorted!

She would just chill today, then maybe join her mum for some Christmas shopping and maybe treat herself to new shoes to match her dress. She wanted a pair of shoes with a thick club heel which was the latest in mod attire, a must-have for dancing.

She would also phone Drew and see what was happening on the social scene. She had been away for a few weeks and felt desperate to get back to the way things were at half term and was looking forward to more parties and just being part of the in-crowd once again.

The shoes were a must, it was a big weekend coming up and there was a big gathering of like-minded mods, all congregating in the centre of town and moving to the in-place, that Saturday night; The Bird Trap, a club, housed in a large empty Victorian building, a short distance from the town centre, just off the main road. A place where the Tamla Motown and soul sounds would reverberate throughout the night.

Clubs such as The Bird Trap didn't open until midnight, so the queue to enter began forming after all the pubs had closed at 11 pm. The queue was orderly and wound around the small streets of back-to-back houses, much to the distress of the residents who were campaigning to close down the all-night club.

Rebecca had the added annoyance of trying to get her parents' permission to allow her to be out all night, but this was just impossible.

There was just no point in going through everything with them to be told 'NO' and of course there would then be arguments.

Skulduggery had to be adopted, pretty damn quick and Rebecca arranged a sleepover with friend Pamela who lived relatively near her.

The arrangement also worked both ways as Pamela's parents were also strict.

Rebecca and Pam were even excited standing in the queue, all the girls with their weekender cases containing their overnight needs, hair and make-up brushes, mirrors, and lipsticks. All were wearing their club-heeled dancing shoes so they could do their twirls and slides to the latest Motown and soul sounds.

The sound of 'Washed Ashore' by the Platters, was blasting down the stairs and out of the front of the premises to the waiting crowd who were all gyrating, as only mods could do. This was Rebecca's favourite Motown song and she couldn't wait to get through the door.

She noticed a boy walking up and down the line. He seemed to be having conversations with lots of the crowd, he was very good-looking with jet black hair and wore a mohair silk suit with a large vent up the back of his jacket. He kept spinning around to the music and his jacket would flare out around him. He was a great dancer; Rebecca could tell that. Then he would get close to people in the crowd and it looked like he was having serious conversations with them.

He accosted Pam and Rebecca and quietly spoke in a Liverpool accent, 'I have black bombers, blues, and brown and clears. Do you want some? They're all good and will keep you dancing all night, I can promise you that.'

The girls declined but he thrust two pale blue tablets into Rebecca's hand. 'Have those on me,' he said, 'I'll see you inside, I'm Ricky, we'll have a dance.' He winked and carried on down the queue.

Pamela was having none of it and she strongly advised Rebecca to do the same, but the little voice inside Rebecca's head was daring her to try the blues and without telling Pamela she slipped them into her mouth and swallowed them. Those would keep her going all night now as Ricky had said.

Inside, The Bird Trap was a huge room with two cages at each side of the stage. In the middle on the stage was the DJ and all his equipment. It was dimly lit, with spotlights on the cages where individuals danced showing off their skills. There were some great dancers and it wasn't too long before the two girls were dancing like professionals.

No alcoholic drinks were allowed, so the revellers made do with soft drinks which could be purchased in an adjoining smaller room. Some had consumed their own alcohol, which they had secreted and brought into the club. This was generally the case. Ricky sought out Rebecca and danced with her for quite a few dances. It was all Motown and soul, so there were no smooches and no togetherness. She wished there was as he was very attractive.

The tablets seem to be working well; she felt totally energised and felt she wanted to dance all night, she never sat down and twirled around the dance floor most of the night even having the floor to herself on a couple of occasions. Sweat was pouring off her and eventually she retired to the bar area and joined a crowd who commented on her dancing.

She was feeling good and now felt part of the in-crowd. She had been accepted. The chat was all about the next weekend's visit to The Twisted Wheel club, in Manchester, a well-known club for mods. They seemed to be taking orders for something or other and were arranging a meet the following weekend prior to going to the club.

Ricky wanted Rebecca to join them and she felt privileged, she liked Ricky and wanted to dance with him again. He took her onto the dance floor, it was nearly seven o'clock in the morning, the club was closing down very soon, but the sound of 'Baby I Need Your Loving' by the Four Tops needed to be danced to.

It was the first slow dance of the evening with Ricky and she relished each moment as she felt his warmth and breath in her ears. They were both perspiring and their cheeks slid against one another's, then he kissed her. *How romantic*, Rebecca thought. He left her wanting more but that was it, thankfully there was always the next week and with Christmas in-between there was so much to look forward to.

It was still dark outside as the crowds left the club and made their way to their usual haunt, a coffee bar near to the bus station in the centre of town.

It was always packed at that time in the morning, the young people laughing and chatting about the all-nighter, before they caught their first buses home.

Ricky had driven off on his scooter with his parka coat flapping open as he gained speed. In fact, there must have been about twenty scooters all parked together outside the coffee bar, this was the mods showing off their style, without a doubt. *So cool*, Rebecca thought.

The thought of going home filled her with dread and the two girls had to wait around a little longer so as not to cause any suspicion with their parents, they would take a light breakfast at the coffee bar before catching their bus home.

Sunday morning at home was always more laid-back, and thankfully as she came through the door all seemed calm; Robert was reading the Sunday paper and her mum was just finishing off her breakfast.

They both seemed pleased to see her and seemingly did not

suspect any wrongdoing, much to Rebecca's delight. She could now see the way forward to the next weekend's meet at The Twisted Wheel. Although she felt very tired, she made herself useful and decided to take Rufus for a walk and then came home and peeled vegetables and potatoes for Sunday lunch without being asked to, which pleased both Mum and Robert. Yes, everything today seemed in harmony *so let's make the best of it all,* Rebecca thought.

Christmas was nearly here, only two days away. Rebecca still had shopping to do and she also wanted to help her mum shop even though they were going to Grandma and Grandpa Catlow's on Christmas Day and the aunts, uncles and cousins would be there too. Rebecca loved it when they all got together, Uncle Clem and Grandpa would tell jokes and silly stories and you just had to laugh at them.

Christmas Eve was her mum's time and they always made steak and chips with onion rings and tomatoes washed down with a bottle of Mateus Rosé wine. Mum liked the rosé but Robert preferred a deep red.

It was good at Christmas because Rebecca was allowed to have either wine or her real favourite, Babycham, sipped gently from a champagne glass just like on the movies. She also felt very light-headed on more than one occasion after Babycham but it was a great feeling and boy, did she sleep well after it.

Christmas morning was great; even Rufus had a bone all wrapped in Christmas paper. He paraded around the room as if he was showing off, before he ripped off the paper and devoured the biscuit bone, which took him no time at all.

Robert and mum liked their presents. Rebecca had bought

her mum a pair of gold earrings with a lovely blue stone in the middle surrounded by what looked like diamonds, but actually were not; diamonds were out of Rebecca's league on her pocket money.

She had bought Robert a hip flask to help him with the very cold mornings when he had to start work early. He was a bus controller and, although he worked in the office, he had to make sure all the London-bound coaches left on time. This meant very early starts and him standing around the draughty bus station, sometimes as early as four in the morning, even in the middle of winter. He was lucky she had bought him anything but she did it to please her mum.

She was adorned with gifts, mostly makeup and clothes. She also got a lovely, leather handbag, one that could be used as a shoulder bag or, by detaching the shoulder strap, as a hand-held bag. It was just the job as she could dance with it wrapped around her and keep her money safe. She was so pleased with all the presents and looked forward to more when she got to Grandma's and Grandpa's.

The large Victorian table at Grandma's was set beautifully.

It was covered with a large, white lace table cloth and another red and white one set over the centre. All the crackers were red and green and there were red napkins at each place setting. Everyone had a water glass and a cup and saucer, Grandma's best bone china ones. Wine wasn't the tipple here, these were working mill folk and their beverage was a bottle of stout or pale ale, which Grandpa had in abundance, in a large crate set next to the piano, in a position where everyone could help themselves.

The ladies generally stuck to cups of tea but the men folk treated themselves; this was Christmas Day after all. The turkey and a ham were carved in the kitchen, by Grandma and Marian. The ham smelt divine and looked beautiful with golden-crusted skin and cloves dotted over the top, giving it a real Christmas fayre fragrance. The turkey was so moist, it was mouth-watering. It had several rashers of streaky bacon over its breasts and legs with butter which was smeared under the skin of the breasts to make it even more succulent.

Everyone sat around the large table all dressed in their best Christmas clothes, with smiles all over their faces. This was truly a superb spread for all to be enjoyed. Grandma always made her own sage and onion stuffing packed full of sausage meat, this was a meal in itself.

Every vegetable imaginable: sprouts, carrots, swede, peas, and cauliflower accompanied the turkey and ham with a rich turkey gravy to top it all off. The meal was consumed over quite a long period, with a long rest before the pudding course, which gave everyone time to watch Her Majesty the Queen give her speech to the nation. Then it was onto the Christmas pudding, with brandy sauce and, if preferred, Grandma's sumptuously decorated sherry trifle and homemade meringues. A platter of Lancashire cheese and biscuits were placed on the large side-board for the family to help themselves to later, if they had any more room in their bellies.

After a long rest and some television Grandpa played the piano. Sometimes he hit the wrong note as he was a little rusty and his hands were not quite as nimble as they might be. Everyone joined in the singing of Christmas carols and some of Grandma and Grandpa's favourites: 'Side by Side', 'Bye Bye Blackbird', not forgetting 'On Ilkley Moor Bar t'at,' Everyone knew the words to these songs and that's how Rebecca learned them.

She poured herself more Babycham than she was allowed, but no one had noticed and she was happy to get up and dance with aunties and uncles accompanied by Grandpa at the piano, in fact she was having a great time with all the family together again.

It was quite late when everyone put on their big coats to wend their way home; they had all booked taxis far in advance of Christmas Day so as to be assured of the journey home. They were all due at Aunt Elsie's and Uncle John's on Boxing Day for another wonderful spread, all homemade by Auntie Elsie.

Boxing Day was also a great day, especially when Auntie Elsie gave Rebecca her fox fur coat as a Christmas present. Aunt Elsie had married Uncle John in the very same fur coat in the 1930s and now fur coats were back in the fashion, all the mods were wearing them. It was also just the right size and the soft, brown fur matched her new handbag perfectly.

Rebecca was over the moon and wore it home that same evening. She would be the envy of the girls now, with her very own fur coat. Thank you so much to Auntie Elsie.

A couple more weeks and Rebecca would be back at school but the coming weekend was foremost in her mind. She had got away with it once and the same strategy would be adopted once again, or so she thought.

It was a bit of a blow when Pamela told her she wasn't going to The Wheel, in Manchester as previously arranged. Rebecca was hopping mad. *Can't rely on anyone*, she thought. She decided she would still tell her parents she was staying at Pamela's house, as Pamela's dad had a car and would pick them up after their night out so her parents wouldn't be wondering how she would get home.

She spoke to Drew as well. Good that he was going, so she arranged to meet him and a few of them would get the coach to Manchester from the bus station.

The bus to Manchester was packed full with 'Wheelers' that two more buses were laid on to accommodate the young people. All the girls carried their overnight weekender cases and total excitement filled the air. The red brick building loomed majestically before them. This was a first for Rebecca, she had heard so much about The Wheel and the Wheelers, as they were referred to. Now she was one of them.

There were crowds hanging around in Brasenose Street outside the Wheel. It was impossible to see where Ricky was, although she kept her eyes skinned for him. She walked down the street amongst the 200-strong crowd queueing to get in until she came to the rows and rows of scooters all lined up displaying their chrome wing mirrors and badges; there must have been four or five mirrors on each scooter.

Ricky saw her in the crowd and approached her from behind, covering her eyes, 'Surprise, surprise,' he whispered in her ear. He then took hold of her hand and off they went together.

'Where we going Ricky?' she asked but without answering he told her not to worry but just to follow him and his two other mates. They got into a mini and drove off, the four of them. It wasn't long and they hadn't gone far when the driver stopped the car in a side street not far from the city centre.

'Wait here,' was the instruction to Rebecca.

The boys got out of the car, it all happened so quick, she heard a smash of glass, an alarm going off, then nothing.

A few minutes lapsed and the three boys returned, threw themselves into the mini and sped off back the way they had come.

Ricky grabbed Rebecca and kissed her hard in the back of the car, he pushed two 'blueys' into her mouth and stared at her saying, 'You're with me tonight, girl. Are you ready to dance?' With that they piled out of the car, back near the club.

Rebecca easily guessed where they had been and what they had done, but she wasn't unduly worried; she was with the in-crowd now, good and proper and they trusted her.

She wasn't disappointed, The Wheel and the Wheelers were her sort of people, she loved being a part of it all. She had made friends now and was accepted into the crowd as was Drew. He wanted to know where she had disappeared to but she replied, 'Ask no questions, tell no lies.'

He laughed reminding her not to miss their bus home.

She was now dancing to Dobie Gray's 'The (I'm In With The) In Crowd', she felt the music as she slid around the floor with Ricky who drew the crowd to watch his spins and she felt proud she was with him. The floor became so full, everyone danced, it was magical, she loved the music and she didn't want it to end.

The crowds fell out onto the street at seven o'clock, when the club closed. It was a cold, frosty morning, even in Manchester, where it has the reputation of always raining, but they never felt the cold, as all were thankful for the fresh air.

Rebecca had been dancing all night, but now the blues were beginning to lose their affect. She knew she was coming down, as they called it, but didn't feel too bad; just extremely tired. She met Drew in Market Street, just round the corner from the club and they went for coffee at the cafe near to the bus station. Breakfast was consumed and Rebecca was starting to feel human again.

She had lost Ricky amid the crowd. That was disappointing as she had no contact number for him and they had made no future arrangements. She knew it was going to be difficult as he lived in Liverpool and she would be leaving home to return to boarding school in a few days, which she was now, not looking forward to after this exciting Christmas break. She made Drew promise to speak with Ricky when he next saw him and to send him her love and tell him how she really enjoyed her Wheel night.

She hoped she would see him soon.

CHAPTER 15

Unbeknown to Rebecca, Robert had thoughtfully decided to collect his stepdaughter from Pamela's to save her catching the bus home. He had had an unusually early start and had finished in plenty of time to collect her.

Not the reception he expected, when he casually knocked on Pamela's front door to be told Rebecca wasn't there and nor had she been all night. Pamela was duly questioned as to her whereabouts and the pressure put on her made her spill the beans. Robert had never heard of The Twisted Wheel and became very angry that Rebecca had lied.

After making his apologies to Pamela's family he continued his journey home to inform Marian of the situation. She would be worried as he was, as they knew not of Rebecca's whereabouts; all they could do was wait until she came home.

It was midday when she eventually walked through her front door looking and feeling totally exhausted. The reception she received was angry and unforgiving. The exchange of words, rang in her ears, but she took no notice and turned directly around and walked out of the door again, leaving the house, she hoped, for the very last time.

She was tired and felt she could not cope with all this aggravation from her mum and Robert, she would go to her sanctuary. There was always a place at Grandma's and Grandpa's, no matter what she had done.

She was always happiest with them and she hoped this would be the start of living with them again in her school holidays. They appreciated her and she could do no wrong.

Robert Tay felt so angry with his defiant stepdaughter, he felt like giving her a good thrashing to knock some sense into her. It was a good job she left the house otherwise it might have been him that was in trouble. He was not the kind of man to comfort his wife and only saw things through his own eyes. He blamed Marian for being too liberal with Rebecca and also blamed her grandparents for spoiling the girl and giving into her every whim. Marian didn't have the energy to argue with him, she just let things lie and hoped the situation would calm down in a few days and Rebecca could come home before returning to school.

Rebecca didn't want to return home and stayed with her grandparents for the rest of the holiday, only returning to the house during the day when Robert was at work, with the sole intention of packing her trunk. She never saw him again before she returned to school.

She hugged her mum and there were tears on both sides, she gave no explanation as to where she had been that Saturday night, nor who she had been with. However, she did tell her mum she had been with Drew, which gave Marian a little comfort.

The father of the girl from school, who lived close to Rebecca, drove her back to school on the Sunday evening, over the cold, dark Yorkshire Moors. It had been a great Christmas apart from getting found out and all the trouble that had caused.

She hoped her mum would be alright thinking *they're probably glad I've gone back to school, as I always seem to cause problems for them*.

The journey back to school seemed very short indeed that night as Rebecca was deep in thought reflecting on the great Christmas holiday she had had. Thoughts of Ricky were going round and round in her head and she was desperately hoping they would meet again when she was next home, although she didn't hold out any hope; he probably went with a different girl every week and would do now seeing as she wasn't on the scene all the time.

She had spoken to Pamela and made it okay with her, she didn't hold a grudge there and they would meet again on her next school holiday when she would tell her all about The Wheel.

It was awful returning to Brantham and Harry not being there, it just wasn't the same anymore. Bernie was still around and things seemed to be a bit more tolerable now; at least the two girls were on speaking terms.

I started the school term this time with everyone else and seem to be included in Rebecca's group of friends although I just sat and listened to them all trying my best not to get noticed.

I always felt I had a friend in Harry. She was a gentler sort of girl and didn't condemn me for the slightest thing I did whereas I always felt on tenterhooks when I was around Rebecca.

Rebecca had had her hair cut very short, she let everyone know she was a mod. Most of us didn't know what a mod was let alone all the fashion and music which mods liked. We were soon exposed to all her Tamla Motown and soul music; she got to play exactly whatever she wanted, as it was her record player which she had brought from home.

I used to get so angry at her, trying desperately to be the centre of attention all the time and I couldn't understand how close Bernie was getting to her especially when they used to be arch-rivals. Bernie was always alright with me, although we would never have been best friends, but she seemed to watch out for me in general. She was certainly a match for Rebecca!

Nothing strange or startling at school, all was much the same as it ever was. The mornings were dark walking down to school as were the evenings. The only bright lights came from the shops in the lower Brantham Village and the highlight of the walk back to Moonacre was the visit to the bakers, that's if pocket money stretched that far. There was no relying on extra cash now. It was always Harry's money from her dad that bought us all cakes on the walk back.

Rebecca had joined Bernie, Helena, and me on our walks to and from school. I learned so much from the girls' conversations which were usually about boys and who they were going out with and the plans for the weekend walks. I wished I could join in. I had never had a boyfriend but the girls kept telling me they would sort one out for me soon, although I didn't relish this one little bit.

There was a boy in our class whom I quite liked, he was very nice and always used to talk to me a break time. The girls kept teasing me about him and to my horror and embarrassment said they would put a word in for me. It was then they first saw my disdain as my reply was, 'That will not happen. If I wish to be involved with anyone, I am quite capable of arranging my own date, thank you.' I quickened my steps leaving them all standing there outside the baker's shop, flabbergasted at my outburst.

I could hear them laughing at my outburst but I think I made my point in a respectful manner, which they probably wouldn't understand, apart from Helena that is. She was a bit more like me, not as forward as Rebecca and Bernie. She was the studious one, a very clever girl in mathematics, physics, and biology but also good fun and caring.

I wondered sometimes how she coped with the other two, but they seemed to like Helena and she always helped them with their homework.

Yes, it seemed as the term went on, that Rebecca and Bernie became bosom buddies. Sometimes I would question Bernie, in a roundabout way as to why she and Rebecca appeared to be so close. One time she answered me with, 'If you can't beat 'em, join 'em. Remember, Eva, keep your friends close and your enemies closer still.' She said this with a smirk on her face and a twinkle in her eye, but I still didn't properly understand her meaning, I just thought she was playing around.

I did get together with the boy, Phillip, he was my age and lived with his family on a farm in Lancashire, not too far from Rebecca. He was a boarder like me and our conversations each break time centred around his farm and his brothers and one sister.

He had dark brown, wavy hair, it was very thick and he told me he had to keep it very short otherwise it would grow like a bush. He was quite broad and had big white teeth, I really enjoyed our conversations and wanted to see more of him. We made an arrangement to meet on our weekend walk at Big Stone the next Saturday.

I couldn't wait to meet him and climb up the stone steps and sit upon the top drinking in the view of the moors above High Brantham.

It was a magical afternoon, cold, but the rain stayed away. A wind blew around the big stone as we sat on the top. He put his arm around me and pulled me into his chest and kissed my forehead; my heart was racing. He was so kind and gentle.

The time went by so quickly. He told me he wanted to be a doctor when he left school but if that failed, he wanted to take over his dad's farm and become a gentleman farmer.

He knew I wasn't really the outdoor type so he said if we were still together when we left school we would spend our time, him on the farm and me doing all the books and making the business work. It was so exciting for him to be thinking of me in that way and when he said, 'Who knows, we may marry' I responded with 'Oh yes, I would really love that.'

These meets were regular; when we could, that is. We soon became an item, and Phil and Eva rolled off everyone's tongue. I was his and I never looked at another boy, he was my best friend I could tell him anything and he always supported me.

Even Rebecca didn't hound me anymore, I had my special friend and everyone knew it.

CHAPTER 16

Things never stay the same, we all know that; people we care about move on and routines that we all get used to change.

It seemed that Rebecca was on her own now more and more, no Harry and no Tony, all in a short space of time. She seemed to have withdrawn into herself slightly and wasn't the fun-loving girl she used to be. I was still friends with her but knew how she could turn on others, therefore I kept her at a distance and my thoughts to myself. I felt this was a good time for me, as I had my rock, Phillip, to talk to and confide in, if anything worried me.

What I didn't disclose to anyone was, that it was me who told on Bernie and Harry, the night they went out. I was sorry I had done it as I thought Rebecca was going with them and wanted to get her in trouble.

I was sick of her bullying me. I wanted to get at Rebecca not at Harry or Bernie. It was very unfortunate that Rebecca didn't go out that night.

A few weeks of the new term passed and we all settled into the routine as usual, Rebecca and I were moved into the senior dormitory, we felt very privileged and were treated in a more grown-up manner by the older girls and the staff.

One Saturday morning, we were all called into Hardy Hall, which was the dining room, for a meeting with the headmistress, the housemistresses and Matron. They explained to us that the senior girls were to move from Moonacre to a large house, a short distance down the road from Moonacre. Sadly, a gentleman on the board of Governors of the school had passed away but had kindly bequeathed his home, Ford House, as a senior girls' boarding house. The chosen few hadn't been informed as yet, but there was lots of excitement and speculation as to who were going to be the first residents after all the refurbishments were completed.

Our dorm captain, Belinda Rudd, was chosen and her friends Pippa Jones, and Penny Hodge who were originally in our dorm, plus all the other girls from the senior dormitory. The Moonacre prefects, who all had their own rooms here on the ground floor, were also moving up to the new house. There were to be lots of changes. Rebecca and I then realised the reason we had been moved into the senior dorm. It wasn't our turn to go to Ford House as yet, but our time would come in the near future.

Then the headmistress and Matron dropped another bombshell and I couldn't believe it, in fact I was astounded; they were making Rebecca a Moonacre prefect commencing at the start of the new coming term. She would be the youngest of all the prefects and was to share one of the prefects' rooms with another girl who was a pig farmer's daughter from Blackpool; a nice, quiet girl who kept herself to herself. Of course, there was always going to be the comment by Rebecca: 'Hope she isn't constantly going to smell of pig shit.'

My only common-sense reasoning for this new appointment was that they wished to give Rebecca more responsibility and to try to keep her on the right side of the fence. I had my reservations. I also had misgivings about the relationship between the two girls.

A few weeks went by and just prior to the summer holidays the girls moved into Ford House. We all went for a visit and were most impressed.

Each room was newly decorated, some with pink walls and other rooms painted in magnolia. In the bedrooms, there was a maximum of four divan beds, each girl had their own dressing table and they would all share wardrobes which had been fitted. It was a warm house, draught-free with central heating and the floor boards had disappeared; the floor covering although not carpet was a soft vinyl, we knew it as lino.

How we envied the older girls! The senior girls and prefects had rooms on the first floor and the not-so seniors climbed up a narrow staircase to the rooms in the eaves. There were more bedrooms on this level, all accessed via the square wrap-around landing. In fact, one room had a rope ladder and trap door down to a first-floor bedroom, probably part of the fire escape system as the fire escape door led out onto metal stairs at the side of the house; a real fire escape, not like the rope ladders at Moonacre. They had to be lowered out of the front windows from the senior dormitory at the front of the building and climbing out of those sash windows was ungainly to say the least, with our bottoms stuck up in the air for all the world to see.

The new cook at Ford was a homely lady, also the kitchen was just like a kitchen in a big house with a table in the middle. The girls could sit round it and talk to Mrs Prindle whilst she prepared dinner. Her meals were delicious, so we were told, she also made cakes and scones for their supper.

I couldn't wait to go up to Ford and nor could Rebecca. Bernie was miffed that Rebecca had been made a prefect, I could tell, although she would never let that be known. She was condescending when in Rebecca's company and it was strange. The disagreements and fighting had ceased and generally things seemed amicable. Nocturnal jaunts also stopped, but weekend walks gladly remained the same. Bernie was still seeing Pete; it appeared to be all water under the bridge to Rebecca, she had crossed that hurdle and seemed disinterested in both Bernie and Pete.

I think Tony's death hurt her a lot, she rarely showed any emotion at all even when we talked about him, she wouldn't open up to anyone. She just used to say she was looking forward to term's end and seeing her friends at home and take up where she left off.

All personal belongings were moved around to the different rooms and dormitories prior to term end so everyone got a taste of their new dorms and where they were to be at the start of the new term.

Prefects' duties were to supervise the cleaning, washing-up and serving teams and assisting the younger girls, getting them ready for the school day. Some were very young and needed this support from the older girls.

Rebecca seemed to take her duties more responsibly and maturely.

The ringing of the first and second morning bells were now

the task of the prefects, they also had a rota for their duties. They also had many more concessions, including staying up later than nine o'clock and they were left to their own devices at weekends choosing to stay indoors if preferred or to take themselves off to the town or the cinema.

Helena Austwick and Rebecca became good friends and they used to team up with their day friends Lynne Barton and Rose Parker. They always seemed to be together and having a laugh.

I was sad when term ended because I wouldn't see Phillip every day; we were always together like an old married couple, never separated. He lived about fifty miles away from me which was a long way when we didn't drive. However, we did arrange to visit each other and met in the old market town of Skipton on one occasion and went to Morecambe also. It wasn't long enough really but was better than not seeing him at all. We still made our plans for our future together and decided it wouldn't be too long before we introduced one another to our families. Maybe on the next exeat day we could all have tea together.

Rebecca's summer holidays went well, probably because she didn't spend too much time in her Robert's company. She had two weeks away with school friend Charlotte Jackson and her parents in Newquay, Cornwall. It was just a small guest house where they stayed, away up the hill overlooking the harbour. They had dinner, bed and breakfast and Rebecca and Charlotte shared a twin-bedded room.

Mr and Mrs Jackson were nice people and they lived near Manchester. Sometimes the two girls would visit each other's houses and stay with each other for a few days in the holidays.

It was there in the harbour area, the family met with another family from Stoke-on-Trent. It was a lovely warm day and everyone was sitting around on the harbour wall. The two families started chatting and so each day of the holiday, they spent time together on the sands and over a drink in the evening.

Rebecca was totally smitten with Geoff, their seventeen-year-old son. She couldn't take her eyes of him. His eyes twinkled and his smile was so attractive with his lovely, even, white teeth and to cap it all he was a mod wearing Levi jeans and braces. Charlotte liked him as well; it was difficult to know who he fancied.

Charlotte had a beautiful face, dark brown eyes, with long, straight dark hair nearly to her waist, a very attractive girl. She was a year younger than Rebecca but they became friends when they were both in the middle and senior dormitories.

Geoff was with his parents and aunt and uncle; they all spoke with a Midlands accent and kept calling the girls 'me duck'. Rebecca was drawn to them all, as they were all so friendly and such fun.

Geoff didn't ride a scooter but drove his father's Ford Cortina and so the three of them spent time going to different beaches together and leaving the adults on the harbour beach. It was such fun and both girls were drawn to Geoff, there were no arguments between them but both liked him a lot.

It was awkward, especially on the last evening together, when they visited the local disco. Geoff kissed Rebecca on the dance floor and wouldn't let her go. He told her he would miss her and wanted to visit her as soon as possible. Charlotte was so upset and could not be consoled by either of them, she took herself off, out of the disco and made her way back to the guest house.

Things were never the same again between the two girls, a fabulous holiday had ended up with one of the girls in tears and a friendship broken. I suppose it was inevitable really, two girls wanting the same boy! The two lovebirds arranged to see each other again, Rebecca would write to Geoff and make the arrangements as soon as possible.

Early the following morning Rebecca skipped her breakfast and headed down to the hotel overlooking Towan Beach to say her goodbyes to Geoff and his family. It was a sad time and Rebecca had an overwhelming feeling she wanted to cry. It was just like the day she was told about Tony, *why was it that everything that was good had to be taken away from her*? She cut a lonely figure as she made her way back up the hill to the guest house.

They were also leaving for the train station soon. It had been a most memorable holiday; the memories would be forever of gorgeous Geoff.

Rebecca was overjoyed when, after a few days at home, she received a letter in the post from him. He didn't hold back and expressed how much he cared for her and how much he needed to see her again. They corresponded regularly and he drove up one Saturday during the day to see her, unbeknown to Marian and Robert.

They spent the day walking in the warm sunshine along The Golden Mile on Blackpool promenade, eating chips and candy floss and he drove her home for seven o'clock, so as not to cause any arguments with her parents.

She had got away with it and made further arrangements to meet Geoff when she was back at school in about two weeks' time. She would have more flexibility now she was a prefect.

The next two weeks of the long summer holidays went by very quickly. She managed to catch up with Drew and Pamela and told them all about her holiday in Newquay, what a place that was. She would love to live there and told her mum of her wish.

It was by pure coincidence that the Tays had decided to pack up all their belongings and start a new life in Cornwall. It hadn't even been mentioned to Rebecca. They had bought a small dairy business and a bungalow near to Newquay. Robert Tay had packed up his job in this northern town and was heading for the south west of England for a new life away from the rat race.

Rebecca seemed very pleased with this news given to her by her mum and in Robert's presence. Grandma and Grandpa were present when the news was forthcoming. They already knew but again were very upset that their daughter and only granddaughter were leaving and moving such a long way away.

So, it was decided that Rebecca would go and live with her grandparents during the short term holidays and only go to Cornwall for the long holidays, an arrangement which pleased her no end. She was free now to do what she wanted; no more

Robert Tay telling her what she could or couldn't do. The adults, were again surprised, as to how she received the news, in fact she didn't care one little bit, she no longer wished to be under the same roof as her stepfather... happy days!

CHAPTER 17

Back at Brantham, Rebecca seemed to settle down very well. She had new responsibilities and she had a new love in her life, even though she didn't see him very much.

She and the pig farmer's daughter seemed to tolerate each other, although she really didn't have much to do with Rebecca. She was a quieter girl, who took her tasks seriously, whereas Rebecca was just one of the girls and discipline was out of the window on her watch.

She seemed to get her mojo back and was always acting the fool like she used to do with Harry. Bernie and she seemed to be alright. I suppose all the disagreements were water under the bridge now!

The room Rebecca shared with Jean, the pig farmer's daughter was small with two single beds, but the headboards were made of wood and not metal like in the other dorms. This was good, because neither girl got any more wood lice in their beds. This was a trait in the senior dorm. Rebecca always awoke with a dead wood louse in her bed; not the most pleasant experience, probably came from the old wooden floor boards.

Around mid-term time things went drastically wrong for her. She upset Matron by talking back. It was a Sunday morning and we were all getting ready to walk down to church in Lower Brantham. We did this every Sunday, walking in a crocodile wearing our best grey Sunday suits and round, blue, fish bowl-shaped hats, with the school crest on the front.

Rebecca had remarked to me, how small the suit had become for her and the white blouse with the Peter Pan collar couldn't be fastened at the neck, nor the cuffs which were half way up her arms. So, she used her initiative and wore her school uniform, much to Matron's wrath. She was ordered to go and change into the suit. Rebecca refused and was sent to her room where she stayed that Sunday.

It was only in the evening she was summoned to Matron's office and told to move her belongings back to the senior dormitory and to hand her prefect's badge back.

Yes, they took her badge back there and then, her time as a prefect was short-lived.

She never did wear the suit again, but nor did she get the freedom at the weekends to do what and go where she pleased, which was a bit of a blow, seeing as Geoff was to visit her on the next exeat day.

She would have to think about that one, especially since her mum had written to the school letting them know she was to go to her grandma's and grandpa's for the short term breaks and Exeat Days.

Grandma came up trumps as she always did and wrote a letter to Matron to tell her she was to be collected by a friend of the family and driven home for the day. Grandma and Grandpa were very happy and knew Rebecca was going out for tea with Geoff and his mother on that exeat day. They had driven up from Staffordshire especially for Rebecca and the three of them spent the day together, having lunch at the special place where she had been with Harry and her parents.

Again, the Sunday lunch was superb and all were glad to spend their time in each other's company. They made arrangements for Rebecca to visit them in the school holidays when she was staying with her grandparents.

The day went too quickly and she spent only a short time with Geoff on his own when they went a walk alongside the River When. There, they talked and kissed. It was all so lovely and Rebecca was very happy.

All too soon they returned to Moonacre saying their good-byes and looking forward to the half term when she was to visit them.

She really liked Geoff and his family and she decided she would introduce him to Grandma and Grandpa in the half term.

Back in the senior dorm yet again, she was sleeping next to Bernie with Helena on the other side. Night-time escapades had ceased since Harry had been expelled, but there were always the weekend walks which still gave the girls a certain amount of freedom to meet whoever they wanted, unbeknown to the housemistresses.

Rebecca was full of Geoff, she never stopped talking about him so it was with some trepidation when Bernie happened to mention Eddie to Rebecca. He was a boy, two years older than the girls, who had expressed an interest to meet up with Rebecca when Bernie was meeting Pete.

Rebecca knew exactly who Eddie was. She remembered

seeing him at the traffic lights on her way home when she was in the old Ford Popular and feeling so embarrassed, as he sat in the back of his dad's Jaguar saloon. He'd had his eye on Rebecca for some time, Bernie told her and wanted to ask her out.

Rebecca couldn't believe her luck, she had always admired him from a far but thought he was out of her league and she knew he had been going out with a Ford girl, who was also a couple of years older than her.

This girl was a well-developed girl, blonde, petite and very pretty. Rebecca wondered what had happened between them. Bernie informed her that Pippa Jones was no longer seeing Eddie, he had ended it and she was very upset, he wanted to go out with Rebecca instead.

She was in two minds as she felt a lot for Geoff but also was smitten with Eddie. He was a hunk and all the girls liked him. Maybe she would agree to meet him the coming weekend just to see what he was like. Geoff wasn't to know and she could choose between them later.

The two arch-rivals with friend Helena went walking together. How times change, one would think they had been best friends for years!

The arrangement was to meet the boys in the field where the barn was. It was a different barn, way up a long lane on top of the hill overlooking Fred's farm from the other side. It was an old stone byre with ladders leading to the hay loft. The barn was in the middle of the field near to Fred's farm and could be approached from a lane leading from near the girls' boarding house and was equally approachable from where the boys would go for their afternoon walk.

In fact, Harry used to see Fred 'tending the flock' as she would say, in the fields, staring through her father's binoculars, which she brought from home for that very thing. Little did Fred know that his every move was being watched as Harry stood on her bed in her baby doll pyjamas, scouring the countryside for images of her darling Fred.

The wind whistled through some of the holes in the drystone walls of the barn, but the hayloft was comfy and mostly draught-free. The three girls climbed the loft ladder and threw themselves down in the hay. They had a great view of the lane and got there at least half an hour before the boys arrived. The mood was light-hearted and full of expectation and many of their questions began with, what if... or what will I do if... as they waited for the boys. They were surprised to see, not just Pete and Eddie, but two more boys from school accompanying them.

They kept as quiet as mice until the boys climbed the ladder then surprised them by throwing straw down on top of them covering them completely. That caused mayhem when all the boys climbed into the hay loft and started to attack the girls the same way, throwing the hay at one another and pulling each other down in the hay. It was very flirtatious and soon the boys were practising their kissing with Helena.

Well, two of them were; it was left for Eddie and Pete to be with Rebecca and Bernie when they all settled down in the hay at each corner of the hay loft.

Eddie was an experienced kisser and showed her how to roll her tongue around his mouth, which she freely and happily did as she was completely under his spell.

This boy was wonderful, there were so many girls in the school who wanted to go out with him, but it was she he was with and that's all that mattered at this moment in time. She knew he had had many girlfriends before her, all older than her so it was a surprise when he asked Bernie to ask Rebecca to go out with him. Pippa became very jealous of Rebecca and unkind words were later exchanged between the two girls but Rebecca was unperturbed, this boy had aroused feelings inside her which she had only experienced with Tony.

She was on cloud nine with Eddie. His hands were rubbing her back and breasts under her size thirty-four-inch bra and black Beatle jumper. Again, she had in her mind her mother's words:

'You will never get a decent boy if you are free and easy, Rebecca.'

Surprisingly, Rebecca adhered to her mother's words and was not prepared to go any further with Eddie; not yet anyway, she wanted to keep this boy. She had previously heard the older girls talking in the dorm at night discussing their sexual exploits and one conversation she remembered was to never go all the way on your first few dates. She was unsure what 'all the way' meant.

What she did like was his tongue in her mouth and how he rubbed her nipples between his fingers and thumbs. He made panting noises and grunting sounds and wanted her to put her hands on his trousers. She could feel him hard as he pushed down on her. They snogged so much her mouth was becoming very sore; her teeth had cut into the inside of her lips and she could taste the blood. It felt frantic, as neither of them came up for air. It was so passionate; another completely different experience to Tony who was considerate and more gentle. But she liked this and would want more. What would she do the next time? She knew what Eddie wanted her to do and she had to be strong and stop him going any further. It was harder than she thought to do this as she so wanted to give in to him.

I bet Pippa Jones, let him go all the way and that's why he dumped her, once he had got what he wanted, she thought. Pippa was a well-developed girl, had it in all the right places so maybe Eddie thought he had conquered her and once he had got what he wanted, it was time to move on.

These thoughts were racing through Rebecca's mind, yes, they were mind games and they were confusing her, what would she do next time? She hoped there would be a next time, she wanted it also. She also wanted to be his friend and proudly talk to him in front of the others at school by the tuck shop, to show everyone they were an item.

But she was with him now and brought back down to earth with someone climbing on the ladder of the hay loft. Thankfully, it was the others going back down the ladder. They called to them both that it was time to go as the walk back to school was longer for the boys and if good timing wasn't kept, they could be liable for being grounded or detention. The two lovers adjusted their attire and pulled hay out of each other's hair. She just hoped they would come back the following weekend.

She loved his smell. He must be wearing aftershave; it was a deep strong fragrance, he told her it was Brut. He had it all over his soft cheeks and she wanted to lick his face and keep the smell with her until she could kiss him again.

She found it hard to focus her eyes against the bright light outside the barn, she was in a very dreamy state and remained that way all afternoon. They went their separate ways and waved to one another as they walked across the fields.

Bernie didn't reveal too much on the walk back to Moonacre, but Helena had got together with Gary, Pete's friend and she had her first kisses with him. She was reeling with excitement and pleaded with the other two girls to let her join them next weekend at the barn.

On returning to Moonacre they tucked into a dinner of Miss Livingstone's hot pot with extra potatoes. They were ravenous and remarked how kissing and doing made one very hungry.

The following day at school Rebecca was suffering; her mouth was sore. She and Eddie had been kissing so hard that her mouth was cut inside causing mouth ulcers. It stopped her from eating and made her feel particularly uncomfortable. *I wonder if his mouth is the same?* she thought. They were together by the tuck shop at morning break, surrounded by many of their friends.

'Same place on Saturday afternoon Becca,' Eddie whispered.

That was sheer joy to her ears, she just hoped the ulcers would clear up in time for the next snogging session.

She spent the week counting the hours until she next could see Eddie and have all those special feelings once again. Yes, it was a happy week at school even though she did have ulcers.

Even the situation back at Moonacre had settled down, she was happy back in the senior dorm and Bernie and she were getting on famously, even talking about visiting each other in the coming holidays.

Bernie had her designs on visiting Cornwall, a place she had never been.

Geoff was a long way from Rebecca's mind although they did correspond with each other, but Rebecca got more letters from Geoff than he did from Rebecca.

She made a passing comment to me and said, 'He's okay for the holidays, but I'm with Eddie right now.' I thought, *how fickle you are, Rebecca.*

CHAPTER 18

It was a good week; Saturday was the day to look forward to as Rebecca was seeing Eddie.

There was no doubt Rebecca's mind was totally elsewhere and not on her schoolwork. She seemed to concentrate periodically but then her mind wandered and she was warned several times for gazing out of the window.

The old barn appeared quiet, they had arrived early and the boys hadn't yet arrived. Fred was out in the fields on his tractor, he must not be seeing Harry this weekend. So, the three girls lay down and waited in the hayloft.

Rebecca couldn't contain herself. She was so excited; she couldn't wait to see Eddie and was constantly talking about him. How she loved him when he wore his Levi jeans, he looked so good in them. Then she would continue to enthuse about how good he smelt, she loved his aftershave and how the fragrance lingered on her skin for hours afterwards, remarking, 'I'm never going to wash again.'

She wasn't to be disappointed this breezy afternoon. Eddie arrived with pals Gary and Pete who were in the same year; they were both two years older than the girls.

'He's with Gary, Helena. Do you like Gary as I think he likes you?' Rebecca said excitedly. Before Helena could answer, Eddie had climbed the loft ladder and grabbed at

Rebecca's legs, pulling her down into the soft hay. They all laughed as the two lovers rolled around in the hay, play fighting. Eddie held her down in the hay with her arms above her head, his body straddled Rebecca's as he gazed down at her. She looked back into his light hazel eyes, he was smiling and his eyes smiled also. He had a beautiful mouth with dazzling white teeth, again he was smiling at her and teasing her with his handsomeness.

Little was said between the two lovers, just his long romantic kisses, rolling his tongue around her mouth said it all. It felt as if he was sucking the life out of her. His hands were feeling her upper body and rubbing her nipples which caused her an unbelievable sensation, he smelt gorgeous and she knew there was no going back. He didn't have to ask her permission; she was a willing participant.

She didn't want him to stop, Eddie knew there was a special place and then, there was no going back. He found the place and she writhed with ecstasy pushing herself against his body, unconditionally.

Helena heard Rebecca cry out, but she couldn't make out what she was saying, so shouted from the one corner of the hayloft, 'Are you alright Becca?' There was no answer, all had gone quiet apart from the sounds of rustling in the hay.

'Come on, Becca. We all need to go now,' Eddie said. She felt dazed, all she wanted to do was hold Eddie close to her for just a few more minutes and smell his body. But Eddie had stood up and was adjusting his clothing and brushing the hay from his hair. The two, looked dishevelled as they descended the loft ladder and held each other close for one last time.

'See you tonight, Eddie, at the film,' Rebecca said as she pulled a piece of hay, which he had missed, from his sandy blonde hair. He kissed her, a peck on her cheek, and with Gary and Pete they were away across the field to the lane which led to the main road.

Rebecca watched them climb the five-bar gate onto the lane and then they were out of sight. She was still reeling and couldn't believe what had happened to her. Helena pulled the hay from Becca's hair and off the back of her denim skirt.

'That's better Becca, but your cheeks are all red, is everything okay? I was frightened when I heard you crying out.'

'Don't worry Helena, all's well, I had a wonderful time.'

'Tell me what you did then, Becca, what was he like? Did you do anything else besides kiss him?'

'What do you think, Helena? Of course, we kissed each other; in fact, we French kissed, you must try it. Anyway, what did you and Gary do?'

'I'll tell you later when we get back. I want to compare notes as you are experienced and I am only learning,' she giggled.

Bernie and Becca were interested to know how Helena had fared with Gary and as the three walked back to Moonacre, Helena told them they had practised kissing each other, so they both would know what to do when that special someone came along. Rebecca smiled when Bernie asked Helena what had happened.

'My stomach is still full of butterflies Bernie, I wanted to stay with him all the time, I didn't want him to leave me this afternoon. I know I love him. Don't you think he is just gorgeous?'

Rebecca kept her information to herself, as Bernie did, but

they made a pact anyway, 'What happens in the barn, stays in the barn.'

Rebecca was pleased because Eddie appeared happy to see her on the Saturday night although they didn't meet, as it was film night, but were to meet on the Sunday afternoon at the barn, so Rebecca wasn't unduly worried. She would look forward to smiling at him across the pews in church and later meet him in the afternoon.

It was a bad Sunday, weather-wise, but after a substantial roast lunch of chicken and all the trimmings, the three girls walked up the lane towards the barn.

Matron told the girls it was too wet to go walking and they were allowed to stay indoors if they wished and amuse themselves reading, watching television, or playing their music. Many senior girls were horrified at this prospect as it was the only time they got any freedom on their weekend walks.

The barn beckoned, there was no contest so rain or shine the girls went on their way, jumping over the swollen streams some of which had burst their banks. Luckily their wellies helped, especially when they were stuck in mud on the other side of a bank. All the three of them could do was laugh and wondered what state they would be in when they met the boys.

The barn was a most welcome sight, all three of them were drenched through to their skin as they climbed the loft ladder. Their outer garments were discarded and hung over the wooden beams to dry, but trousers, jumpers and shirts appeared to steam dry on their own through the heat of the girls' bodies.

A short time later the boys arrived, they were also very wet but the mood was light-hearted and all sat round in the hay loft talking and laughing. They shared the bottles of cider which the boys had brought, all taking it in turn to drink from the large glass bottles.

Eddie was most attentive to Rebecca which she was delighted about, as it had crossed her mind, he may not want to see her anymore.

But all felt good, it seemed they were an item now and he was treating her as such. They talked about her going with him on the next exeat day to visit his home in Blackpool on the Lancashire coast. He kissed her tenderly and stroked her face whispering, 'I really like you Rebecca,' and Rebecca just felt marvellous at hearing this. She would be the envy of all the girls now, but more importantly she was so happy he felt as she did.

They spoke quietly to each other all that afternoon. He spoke of his father's engineering business and how it didn't really matter to him about passing exams, as he was to follow his siblings into the family business.

She told him she was undecided about a job for the future; maybe it would involve animals as she adored all animals.

He told her he liked The Beatles and The Searchers and also a group called The Pretty Things, who Rebecca had heard of because Pete had liked them. He didn't understand what being a mod entailed but seemed quite impressed when she told him about the all-nighters she been to and how they danced till dawn and then breakfasted at the local coffee bars. He intended to drive as soon as possible, he was nearly seventeen and said he had been driving off-road for months in his own car, practising for his road test.

This thought stayed with Rebecca as she realised this would be a good move for her, to pass her driving test and get her own car. Complete independence was the way forward and then she could go anywhere she pleased.

It was Eddie who also introduced her to the interest of potholing.

He was a member of the school's outdoor activity group which spent a few weekends pursuing this specific activity, usually on Saturdays, when the weather permitted. The school group would visit several caves in the limestone terrain on the Yorkshire moors.

All were equipped with helmets, torches, and life jackets so nothing was left to chance with this dangerous pastime.

Rebecca remembered the list which was always pinned to the school notice board asking for pupils who were interested to add their names. There were never any girls' names, as it was thought to be a sport just for the boys. However, other names were added, by some comedian, such as Val Doonican, Elvis Presley and Peter Paul and Mary.

Her thought was, maybe she should take this sport a little more seriously especially as Eddie was part of the group. She mentioned it to Bernie who seemed in agreement. The next fell walk she went on she would speak to the instructor about joining. Mr Grey was the physics teacher but he also took the boys potholing and a mixed group on fell walks.

Mr Grey was in his forties with a mop of grey hair, pockmarked skin and a very deep, gruff voice. He seemed quite a shy man especially when girls spoke to him. He was a housemaster and definitely more used to dealing with the boy boarders who all really liked him. He never lifted his hands to them, not like some of the other masters who seemed to enjoy a bit of corporal punishment. This was according to some boy boarders of course, who apparently could tell one or two tales about their punishments!

Rebecca always thought Mr Grey should have been called Mr Green because of the green jacket he always wore. Every day he wore the same old, green wool jacket, the back of which was splattered with ink from fountain pens. As he walked up and down by the benches in the physics laboratory, pupils would flick the ink from their fountain pens onto the back of his jacket. That's probably why he always wore the same one; it was not worth getting another one ruined.

How do I know this?

I saw this happen with my own eyes on a regular basis, Rebecca also being one of the culprits.

Then there were always huge giggles and laughter afterwards. I think a lot of the class enjoyed Mr Grey's lessons as it was always quite laid-back but his jacket was thoroughly ruined. I don't think he had a wife otherwise she would have probably made him change it from time to time.

Pete was also a member of the group and he kept trying to get Bernie to place her name on the list also. So, for the next fell walking group activity Rebecca and Bernie put their names down in order to speak to Mr Grey about their intention to join the potholing and caving team.

There were about twenty of them who all piled into a hired coach.

Rucksacks took quite a lot of the room on seats, filled with packed lunches which had been specially prepared in the school kitchen. Lettuce and spam sandwiches with a chocolate sandwich biscuit, accompanied with a Rich Tea and the pupils' own flasks filled with hot tea.

Ingleborough, was the climb this day, the second highest mountain in the Yorkshire Dales at 2,372 ft when accessed from Ingeleton at its foot.

Good attire was certainly necessary for this hike and Rebecca was fully kitted out in her walking boots and warm jumpers and her cagoule.

She wanted to give a good impression that she was serious about joining the potholing group.

It was a good, still day. Although rain was forecast, the clouds looked kindly down upon them with no apparent rain clouds. They were to climb to the summit and return on the circular route over Ingleborough Common. It was a hard walk, although the limestone scenery was spectacular and there were far-reaching views over the Yorkshire Dales and as far as the Lake District. It was quite steep up to the summit, a distance of about 100 yards. Sadly, the view from the summit wasn't great due to a mist that had descended over the top of the mountain.

On reaching the summit, each in the group unpacked their lunches and sat around swapping stories, having felt an achievement of actually getting to the top and feeling good about themselves. Ingleborough is one of Yorkshire's three peaks, it is the second highest and affords wonderful panoramic views of Whernside, Pen-y-ghent and as far as Morecambe Bay and around the Lake District, when there is no mist at the top that is.

Rebecca and clan had a chuckle at a place called Humphrey Bottom which is on the way to the summit.

Rebecca decided now was the time to put her plan in motion. She was going to ask Mr Grey about potholing. She was only going to ask him for a laugh at first, but the more she thought about it, the more it appealed to her and it was something she and Eddie could do together.

She approached Mr Grey who was surrounded by other pupils all munching on sandwiches and drinking hot tea. She offered him a slab of her chocolate and Kendal mint cake, a must to have and nibble on up a mountain, which was gratefully received.

'Sir,'

'Yes Rebecca,' Mr Grey answered, as he bit into the pork pie covered in cranberries on top. *I bet he didn't get that from school canteen*, Rebecca thought.

'Can we go potholing, can us girls go potholing?'

'Yooo pot 'olin', Miss Tay, I don't think so,' he replied mockingly in his deep gruff voice, grinning from ear to ear. As if to say, you're joking with me! At least that's what he hoped. 'I wouldn't trust you to get me out of a fix; more likely cause one'! he added, with a wry smile across his face. And with that everyone laughed.

'But why can't girls go potholing, sir? Why is it just the boys… and Elvis Presley (as was written on the notice board)!' she replied. This went over his head!

'No girl has ever showed the slightest interest in potholing, Miss Tay, and I have never been asked that question. It just doesn't seem a sport for girls,' he stated.

'Well, sir, me and Bernie Morrow are interested so please will you consider us for your next outing? We are willing to do all the training needed and all the safety aspects if you are willing for us to join the group.'

He was surprised at the seriousness of her, as all he ever saw was a mischievous individual who wasn't really interested in very much apart from sport. He knew she was the sporty type.

Well, that was it, the question had been put and Rebecca was now happy, she had at least planted the seed in Mr Grey's mind and she could see no reason for them to be declined a space on the next outing.

She and Bernie might have been interested in potholing, but it certainly was not *my* idea of fun. As I have said, I would much rather read a book or watch a film, I am not the energetic type. But we all know why they wanted to get in on the act; anything to be with the boys. That was my cynical thought anyway!

The walk down the mountain was easier and took half the time it had taken to climb up. They passed the huge cave called Gaping Gill. Mr Grey explained he had been down the huge cave and it was an exhilarating experience. He explained the pothole was a depth of ninety-eight metres, with the stream, Fell Beck, flowing into it and that it was Britain's largest cave. He also said it was very dangerous and you had to be experienced to even attempt a descent into this cave.

They continued back towards the Ingleborough cave and then along to the village of Clapham where the bus was waiting for them.

They had walked in a group with Eddie and Pete all of the day and had such fun that Rebecca hardly remembered the walk back. She watched Eddie, how he walked, how he ate his sandwiches and how particular he was using his handkerchief as a napkin. She liked that.

The clothes he wore, looked expensive although he said they were hand-me-downs from his older brothers. In fact, Rebecca thought everything about him was wonderful.

Let's hope she wasn't going to be disappointed, that would be real heartache to her.

Straight to the back seat on the bus and Eddie and Rebecca snuggled down in the corner away from any prying eyes of Mr Grey and Miss Rayne, the games mistress. They must have snogged all the way back to Moonacre where the girls were dropped off, before the rest of the journey down to school.

The girls slept well that night and awoke totally refreshed, although both had aching legs. But today was Sunday so they could relax a little as it was evensong that night which gave them the morning free.

Rebecca decided she would find out all she needed to know about potholing and caving, to show she meant business and she thought about being the first and most courageous girl in the school to go down a pothole. She wasn't going to tell Bernie this. She still didn't like the girl but they were getting on okay now and that suited them both.

Eddie had explained to her that potholing and caving was a serious pastime, not a recreation to be taken lightly as lives could depend on it.

It took stamina and guts, as some difficult situations could develop and one had to keep a cool, calm head in order to resolve the situation. Rebecca liked this side of Eddie, the more serious side. He was a boy who had everything, she thought: good looks, clever and caring. She was so proud he wanted her and not any of the older girls.

Pippa Jones had started to ignore Rebecca. She used to be very friendly towards, her but now she was obviously jealous. Pippa and Eddie had been an item for quite some time and even spent their holidays together when away from school. It was a good job she had moved up to Ford House, as now the two girls' paths rarely crossed. She made it known that Rebecca had stolen Eddie from her and would never forgive that; that was water off a duck's back to Rebecca; she wasn't worried in the least and would deal with her if need be.

There was no chance to speak with the boys that Sunday evening but smiles across church pews gave Rebecca a warm feeling inside, she was so excited at seeing Eddie even if it was only in church. She would have to wait until tomorrow when they would meet outside the tuckshop at break time with their friends, when the discussion would no doubt be about their walk to Ingleborough and any future caving and potholing.

Eddie always seemed to have money for the tuck shop. Rebecca had spent hers already, but he shared the bars of chocolate with her and she shared the goodies she made in the domestic science lesson that day.

She had been reprimanded by the domestic science teacher for throwing pastry across the room at Lynn Barton and Rose Parker. She got a complete dressing-down from the tall, slim, bespectacled teacher, telling her to grow up and not be so childish, but the girls didn't take the telling-off too seriously and as soon as her back was turned, another great lump of dough hit Helena Austwick on the back of the head, thrown by you know who. Side-splitting stuff!

After school, the apple tarts and fruit scones were dished out to Eddie, Pete, and other boy boarders but the remaining freshly baked goods were consumed on the long walk back to Moonacre by Helena, Bernie, and Rebecca. They were so full that they hardly had any room left for their evening meal of lamb stew... but surprisingly enough, they managed to eat all that was placed in front of them.

Watching this group walk up the road you would have been hard-pressed to realise that two of the so-called friends had been arch-rivals a few months earlier. Now they were all laughing and joking together and sharing each other's personal experiences. They even stopped to say hello to Joss and made goofy teeth gestures at the poor animal; but he didn't seem to mind.

I walked up the road slightly behind them with Joan Digby, I was safe with Joan; she was most likely to have been the one ridiculed between the two of us.

I began to hate the girls; Helena was just as bad associating with them. I always felt she was slightly afraid of them and adopted the stance as Bernie said, 'If you can't beat 'em...'

Chapter 19

It would seem that Rebecca and Eddie were all loved up. They saw each other at school as per normal and then visited the barn most weekends; their only time together when they could be completely on their own.

Rebecca felt this relationship was long-term and felt happy, not wanting to think about others; even Geoff was way down her list.

Eddie talked about her visiting him in the school holidays, and although she wanted to, it was going to be difficult, as she had promised Geoff and his parents she would visit them in Stoke.

However, she would worry about that when nearer the time.

I was happy enough and was still great friends with Phillip. He was my rock and I could talk to him about anything. I let him know about my feelings towards the girls and he used to tell me, 'Things never stay the same and this situation with them is no different.'

Those kind words comforted me.

After much deliberation and by that, I mean several meetings between Joss and Peg and other staff members of staff, Mr Grey excitedly announced in assembly about a week later that girl pupils could be included in outings when the caving and potholing group next met. He did add that he was very sorry to say that Elvis Presley would not be attending as he was 'rocking in gaol'. Think Mr Grey must have had the joke explained to him! There was huge laughter in assembly that morning.

However, there was a proviso, that the girls should undergo rigorous training and training in safety procedures prior to the next outing. It was explained to them that if they did not perform and attain the correct level required then they would not be included in the trip.

Rebecca was elated with this decision and the smiling faces looking at her in assembly made her feel proud. She had persuaded the staff to allow the girls to be involved. Some gave her a pat on the back as they filed out of the assembly hall. Eddie was well chuffed to say the least.

'Well done girl,' he said, 'Really didn't think that old stuffy lot would agree to it. Good old Mr Grey, what a decent chap he is!'

Rebecca agreed with Eddie and vowed to try her hardest to pass all the trials and safety procedures necessary. She wanted to be good at this and she knew it was well within her capabilities.

As a result of her new-found adulation, she endeavoured to recruit more girls, besides herself and Bernie, to join them in learning and experiencing caving and potholing on a purely basic level. Some were very apprehensive but Rebecca's persuasive limited insight into it and the fact that training would be given, during the evenings down in the school hall, persuaded others. It would also give the boarders a chance to escape the rules and regulations of boarding house monotony, so she soon mustered up a few intrepid would-be cavers.

Yes, I also agreed to be part of the group but only because Phillip suggested I should. He was a member and he would help me to understand the information, rid any doubts I might have and set me on the right path.

Rebecca was very surprised when I added my name to her list, her sarcastic comment was, 'Oh! shock and awe!' but I had expected some negative comment and wasn't disappointed.

The head boy, Barry Harker, a reasonably experienced caver who was a member of the Ingeleton Cave and Potholing Club, and Mr Grey gave us our first insights into the training and the safety aspects.

From what they were saying about how physically fit one had to be I was having serious doubts about my capability. Strong shoulders, upper body strength, good body control and balance. I had none of these but I stayed for the lecture and sat with Phillip who also knew I would be doubting myself. A quick squeeze of my hand from Phillip made me smile back at him.

The instructors then showed us some of the apparatus required for the task: the ropes and how they threaded through the devices to ascend and descend and how they would belay each other up and down the rocks. It was also important to wear the correct clothing, good boots, and inner and outer clothing. It was cold down in the caves, so the clothing worn must be flexible and not cumbersome as movement through narrow and some very low spaces was inevitable.

Both Barry and Mr Grey expected fitness and maturity from all their pupils as these tasks were not for the faint-hearted. They also reiterated that this sport could be extremely dangerous if procedures were not followed correctly and how important it was to be able to rely on one another! We all left the assembly hall chattering and somewhat enlightened as to the new sport for which we had volunteered.

We were allowed to jump on the bus back to Moonacre that evening as it was getting dark. There would be another training session in the middle of the following week before half term, then it was up to each individual person to work on their body fitness and stamina.

We would be tested on return after the school holiday.

The holidays came all too quickly for Rebecca; she and Eddie seemed to be inseparable. They said they would contact each other during half term but nothing was specifically arranged except that they would see one another.

Geoff's mother had been in touch with Grandma to ask her permission for Rebecca to visit and Grandma had given her permission. This was arranged before Rebecca had arrived home from school.

She had a lot to fit into the ten days' holiday. She had to help her mum with the packing for their new life in Cornwall, go to Geoff's and also visit Eddie. She would do her best to accommodate all this. Grandma wouldn't divulge her itinerary so that was most helpful.

We all said our goodbyes outside the school entrance as car after car stopped at the top of the driveway. I was going home that day with Phillip's parents to stay a few days and then go to my home for the second half of the break.

Robert didn't collect Rebecca; she went back to Grandma's

with the school friend whose father drove them. He and Robert took it in turns to collect the girls, but this time they were picked up outside the school gates in a very nice motor, not an old borrowed rust bucket.

Eddie left with his brother and sister, he waved from the back of the car.

Grandma and Grandpa were delighted to welcome Rebecca home and were looking forward to hearing all her tales and updates from her school term. Marian was to call at the house to see her and the following day they would go to the house and continue packing.

Marian wanted to know what they had of Rebecca's to take to Cornwall with them or did she want all her things left at grandma's.

They were all four together again, a first for a long time. They ate a great home-cooked meal of pork chops, cabbage, jacket potatoes followed by Grandma's homemade roly-poly jam pudding and custard. Rebecca was delighted to be back and the chatter was non-stop about the fell walking and the up-and-coming cave exploration, which was received with caution. She kept away from the subject of how she was doing, revising for her examinations. It would be Robert who would be asking those uncomfortable questions when she next saw him.

However, maybe he'd have forgotten all about her, as his attention would be totally consumed with the move and his new life in Cornwall. She hoped so anyway!

Full as a flock bed, as Grandma used to say, after a good meal, they all went to bed, well fed and watered. Back sharing her old bed with mum and the comforting sound of the cistern refilling made her fall into a deep sleep.

The next day, the two awoke to the smell of bacon cooking and the sound of Grandpa raking the coals in the grate before he made up the fire. After washing and dressing they made their way down the steep stairs and sat down at the large, square, oak table in front of the coal fire and consumed the hearty breakfast which was put in front of them. This amount of food would keep them going all day.

Robert was to come and collect them, as it was quicker than the two-bus journey especially when things needed doing and quickly at that.

There were meter readings to be taken and the house had to have a thorough clean before they left it to the new owners, who were due in the day after. They were all to sleep at Grandma's on the last night before their very early start and a journey of over 400 miles to the south west of England.

Rebecca thought about this new life for her mum and hoped so much that she would cope okay and would meet new friends and take life a little easier. She also hoped Robert Tay would be kinder to her mum, but she was unsure about this. Life would probably be okay for mum as long as Rebecca stayed out of his way and spent most of her time up north or at school.

They set off at four o'clock the following morning. It was still dark outside. Rufus was put in the back of the Morris 1000 van which Robert had purchased and Marian had learnt to drive, so they could both share the driving on such a long journey.

Rebecca had a knot in her stomach and she felt amazingly sad on this dark morning.

She had never felt like this, even when she was leaving home for school, but this was so final, to see Mum and Rufus leaving her and not to see them for a long time; well, at least until the summer holidays. She hugged her mum and Rufus and then walked back into Grandma's house, before the van pulled away. She wanted to explode and cry, but wouldn't let *him* see her cry, she would keep her crying for later.

The hatred welled up inside her, *taking away Mum and Rufus*, she said to herself, the most important things in her life. She bit her cheek and brought blood, in order not to cry.

Grandma had a tear or two but Grandpa was just very quiet, he hadn't told one of his jokes all morning, which was unusual. He always had something light-hearted to say. All he said was, 'He'd better have learned to keep his hands to himself.'

He had never hit Marian, just his wicked stepdaughter who, he would say, had pushed him to his limits.

CHAPTER 20

Rebecca spent the long day with her grandparents at the house. She had no incentive to do anything else, so with Grandma they made homemade cakes and ginger biscuits, Rebecca's favourites. It felt homely and warm at Grandma's; always a safe haven. The two of them chatted away about different things and she confided in Grandma and told her that she felt a load had been taken off her shoulders now Robert had left.

They discussed the incident on holiday but not the detail of the damage to the car by the spoon, that would be her secret.

Although an upsetting day, Rebecca was so tired she slept well and awoke refreshed. She felt surprisingly positive and knew she had to start to organise the rest of the half-term break or it would be over before it had even started.

She read the letter from Geoff which she had received the day before but because of all the turmoil hadn't had time to read it properly and digest it. The plan was, he would drive up to Grandma's and collect her the following day. She was ambivalent about the whole visit to Geoff's. She talked it over with Grandma and said how she felt. She could tell Grandma most things and knew she would not be judged. It was too late to cancel Geoff's visit so she packed her weekender case ready for the following day. Geoff was a decent young man Grandma had said and added, 'And you just may have a nice time'

The following day Geoff arrived at Grandma's in his parents' blue Ford Cortina. He stayed for a sandwich and a cup of tea and couldn't refuse the array of cakes Grandma had produced. They both indulged in the homemade custard tarts and Grandma made a little parcel of jam tarts for the journey to Staffordshire.

It took them about an hour and a half to reached Geoff's house in the potteries, a house quite similar to Grandma's but with an inside toilet.

Rebecca was to sleep in a double bed in Geoff's room next door to Geoff's parents. Geoff was sleeping downstairs on the settee. He said he didn't mind as long as Rebecca was comfortable.

She said she could only stay for a couple of days as she had schoolwork to complete and needed any time she had left to see her cousin and aunties and uncles, who were going to Grandma's the coming weekend.

Then she was back to school on the Sunday night.

They ate that night with Geoff's parents. The conversation was mostly about her parents leaving for Cornwall. She could tell they didn't approve; firstly, sending her off to boarding school and then as soon as she arrived home for a holiday they had packed up and left.

They didn't say so in so many words but Rebecca could read between the lines.

This family must have felt empathy for her as they couldn't do enough to make her stay any better. She felt truly looked after by all three of them and even when Geoff's aunt and uncle visited, they too seemed to be happy she was here. They talked more about the future and even included Rebecca in their next holiday plans, to Cornwall of course, where they had all met. Geoff's mum suggested in the summer they would very much like to meet her parents when the family visited Cornwall.

'We can all travel together and can stay in a hotel. You can stay at your parents' house,' his mum stated.

Rebecca's thoughts about future arrangements and forward planning were falling on deaf ears. She was unsure about her feelings and didn't want to be pushed into future arrangements which she couldn't and wouldn't want to keep.

His mother, although a nice lady, was very pushy and she knew her parents would be totally against meeting Geoff's family. Rebecca was too young to get seriously involved with one boy. Her mum used to tell her she must never pair off alone with any boy, let alone go on holiday with the family.

She willed the next two days to go as quickly as possible as she felt this pushy woman would have her married off before she could say, 'I do not!' However, she just kept smiling and saying the right things and laughing at the right time and complimenting Geoff's mum on her food and let the other stuff go over her head.

She and Geoff stayed up quite late in the sitting room where Geoff was to sleep. They talked a long time and listened to Tamla Motown and soul tracks from his numerous record collection. They kissed a lot and he told her how he had missed her and that he wanted to see more of her. *This is going to be difficult*, she thought.

She really like Geoff; he was a handsome young man and had a good job. But it was Eddie who had really stolen her heart and she wanted to make a go of it with Eddie. She was not interested in any other boy and would prove it to Eddie when she returned to school. This visit had proved to her how she felt and all she wanted to do was to go back to Grandma's and to stop pretending.

The following day was spent sightseeing in the wide, open spaces of Shugborough Hall and gardens. They walked around the luscious estate and afterwards enjoyed a cream tea at the little cafe in the grounds. It was a most enjoyable day.

That evening after a couple of drinks in the local pub Geoff took Rebecca to the local in-crowd dancing venue called The Place in Handley. It was a night of Motown and soul music and in between the dances a few drinks of vodka and lime kept Rebecca happy.

The following day it was decided she would return to Grandma's in the late afternoon. She would get the bus back; it would take longer but she just wanted to be on her own with her own thoughts.

After a late cooked breakfast, she packed up her weekender, and said her farewells and thank yous to Geoff's parents. Geoff saw her off at the bus station. He kept trying to make arrangements as to when and where they would see each other again, but Rebecca said she would write to him and they could make any future arrangements then. She knew she would not see him again and reflected on their conversation on the bus back. How Geoff had said he wanted marry her in the future but wouldn't ask until he had something to offer her.

How silly, she thought. She was far too young to even think about settling down and her mum would go crazy. That was a near miss, better off and away from all that commitment. The bus journey felt just like a ride to freedom.

Grandma and Grandpa were pleased she was home, she could join them, her cousins and aunties and uncles for Sunday tea. She felt a great burden had been lifted from her shoulders and was also extremely happy to receive two letters in the post from Eddie when she arrived back. She would have to explain to him she had been away helping with the move and had only just received them a few days before returning to school.

The next few days of the holiday she would be able to go and select her new walking boots and other attire needed for the potholing and caving expeditions with the school.

This was a serious task for her, and she intended to be as good as any of the boys in her school. She would show Mr Grey she meant business and was not taking matters light-heartedly as she did in previous escapades when she was known to act the fool.

Grandma and she went shopping the next day. They sat at the front of the bus going into the centre of town and laughed, chatting about different things, and remembered Grandpa's shopping spree, when he had bought the rug with blue in it. They were sitting at the front of the bus and so was Grandpa when he suddenly saw the blue colour in the rug.

Grandma reflected, 'I told him any colour but blue.' They laughed out loud and the other passengers also laughed at them laughing.

The outdoor shop was very near Robert Tay's old office. Rebecca selected a good quality pair of Gore-Tex walking boots in a dark grey colour, waterproof over trousers and a couple of pairs of warm socks.

She had other pieces of outdoor clothing which would suffice for the time being. She would see how it all went before spending more money. If she progressed further, she might require other equipment.

Grandma and she treated themselves in the market hall. They sat down for their lunch of meat and potato pie and peas followed by sponge pudding and custard.

After the shopping and luncheon, they slowly window shopped their way back to the bus station and caught the bus home, both of them full up with food and vowing never to eat another morsel for the rest of the day.

The rest of the week seemed to go slowly enough. She wrote to Eddie and explained why she hadn't visited him during the half term.

She hoped he would understand this. She told him she had bought new attire for the potholing outings and was looking forward to seeing him very soon.

She thought it a good idea to wear her boots around the house to break them in, before she took part in any activities at school.

A few days later she was back in the girls' boarding house after the journey across the moors with her travelling companion and her pal's dad.

They had collected Rebecca from Grandma's and were waved goodbye, for yet another part of the school term.

CHAPTER 21

I had spent some of the half term with Phillip's family at the farm. I was introduced to his parents and brothers Jack and Chris, who were lovely and most welcoming. He had an older brother who was also a farmer. He had a lot of responsibility running the day-to-day workings of the farm, which took a lot of pressure away from their father. His mother was a very nice lady. She wasn't just a farmer's wife she actually was the business brain of the family and kept all the books up to date.

It was a happy family time. I was shown around the farm and informed about how they kept records of all the breeding cows and how they could trace their offspring's lineage way back. It was most interesting. I secretly thought that maybe one day I would be able to call myself a farmer's wife and be in this happy family environment. Their life seemed just perfect and Phillip was so happy to be amongst them and on the farm.

I can dream!

Jack drove us back to Moonacre that afternoon. He dropped me off and then continued down to school to drop Phillip at the boys' boarding house. Jack had to get back to the farm as all the cows would need milking. I realised farming was not for the faint hearted. Up early in the morning, late evenings and then the whole procedure repeated again the following day. I am sure he must be exhausted at the end of each day.

It was a lovely break away but back to reality now and all thoughts of me being a farmer's wife pushed away.

Along with others, Rebecca arrived back early evening. As only she could do, she gushed into the dormitory so full of herself and talked about what she had done in half term. We all had to listen to her story of Geoff and her visit to his home and the saga of her parents leaving for Cornwall. If ever there was a narcissist, she was a fine example. I felt my cheeks redden but not through embarrassment, I was waiting to explode... she was making me so mad.

If she had started on me with her nasty ways, I think I would have been ready to clout her one. That is how I was feeling. It seemed the week I had had and all the lovely thoughts and experiences were suddenly taken over by this narcissistic girl.

I unpacked my case and put everything away and walked out of the dormitory. I made no comment as I left, but felt the stare from her, boring into my back. I wasn't going to give her the satisfaction of me listening to her and pretending to like her any more. I was surprised at myself. I calmed down later and thought I mustn't provoke, as life at Moonacre went on and we all had to live together. I would keep out of her way as much as possible.

Everyone knew she was head over heels in love with Eddie so why was she telling all and sundry about her visit to Geoff's during the break. I am sure Eddie wouldn't like that if he knew!

She and Bernie seemed best of pals but maybe that was all pretence on Bernie's part and she took the stance, 'If you can't beat her, join her!'

All of Rebecca's new attire for the outdoor pursuits was spread over her bed and being admired by some of the other girls much to Rebecca's delight. Bernie had some items also; it appeared the two of them were comparing notes and clothing ready for their next outing to Ingleborough and the caves. They both seemed very serious about learning the new sport. The chat in the dormitory that night was predominately about the potholing and when their first instruction would be. Rebecca said she would approach Mr Grey tomorrow and see what arrangements he had decided upon.

It was raining the first day back, even Joss was in his stable sheltering from the wind and rain. The girls all dressed in their blue gabardines and blue berets, sauntered along the long walk down to school. It was a long line of blue, none of them rushing even though it was raining.

Eddie was looking around in assembly to see if Rebecca had arrived. They both smiled at each other, their friendship was obviously still on at this time but we will see what happens in the future as Rebecca was so fickle.

After assembly prayers and the bible reading by a sixth form pupil, the notices were read out by Joss. There was to be a fixture for the girls' netball team at home this coming Saturday and therefore a practice after school on Thursday evening. The boys' first eleven football team had an away fixture at Kirby Stephen that Saturday also. An early start for them as they had some way to travel for that game.

Rebecca was waiting to hear about the fell walking and caving notices and whether they would be included with rest of the team. The first instruction would be the coming Friday evening after school in the double classrooms and the boys wishing to attend must write their names on the notice board. Rebecca's ears picked up on this, no mention of the girls then! Just boys adding their names to the list.

She was incensed by this and couldn't help herself. In front of the whole school, she stood up and spoke:

'That's not correct sir!' Joss removed his spectacles to the end of his nose, he always did that, probably for effect more than his vision.

He scanned the hall and asked who had so rudely interrupted him, Rebecca put up her hand. 'Sir, it's me Rebecca Tay, we, well us girls were told we could participate as well as the boys, we will do just as well as them. We should be allowed to learn and then go on outings with the boys as well.'

'It is not a sport for girls, Rebecca, and it is not a frivolous participation, as you would most likely treat it, Rebecca Tay,' he answered.

There was a subtle titter which spread around the assembly hall.

I added to that laughter. I was so pleased she had been surprised with the headmaster's remarks after all the chat in the dormitory last night.

'If you wish to discuss this further, Miss Tay, I will see you in my office after assembly, and in the meantime, I thank you not to interrupt me again.'

They filed out of the assembly hall row by row. She was raging and ready to go to Joss's study and confront this injustice.

It seemed ages before Joss arrived back at his study. She wasn't too bothered as she was missing her French class and she didn't like French, or the teacher.

'Come in Rebecca and sit down and tell me your thoughts regarding all this,' Joss said.

'Sir, I have bought all my clothes and boots ready to start the caving. I think I will be good at it, but us girls need a chance to show what we can do,' Rebecca stated vehemently. 'I know what you think of me, I will work hard to be good at this as I will enjoy the challenge. I won't be frivolous ever again, just give us girls a chance and we will show you we can be just as good as the boys.'

She surprised herself that she didn't hold back and Joss seemed lost for words.

'The headmistress may not agree with you, Rebecca, and what she says, goes, about you girl pupils,' Joss replied.

'Please sir, please will you speak with her and persuade her to let us join, we will prove you wrong,' Rebecca added, and was then dismissed, without an answer.

Rebecca and pals all met up next to the tuck shop at the first break, all swapping stories about the half-term holiday and of course giggling and chatting about the confrontation in assembly. All were praising her, which she just lapped up. I was there with Phillip and could hear all that went on.

We all had money to spend at the tuck shop, as it was the beginning of the rest of the term and we all had spending money from home. By the end of term, boarders would be cadging sweets and chocolate from the day pupils as they always had their daily allowance.

But just now we all had loads of sweets which filled us all day.

Lunch was horrible at school; the potatoes were made at

about eleven o'clock in the morning and kept warm until one. They stank to high heaven and even I couldn't eat the lunches, so tuck shop food had the edge.

Rebecca was told by Joss, that the ultimate decision regarding the girls being allowed on the caving and potholing outings, would solely be the headmistress's decision and he would announce it in assembly very soon.

Eddie and Rebecca chatted all break, they even held hands and he told her how proud he was of her and so hoped the heads would allow the girls to join.

Before the decision was announced Rebecca collaborated with the girls to put their names on the notice board list and not to put on any jokey names, as they would have normally done. She was on a mission and for once in her, life a serious one. Even I was persuaded to add my name. Phillip had added his name so that was the incentive for me. At least I would see more of him. Rebecca remarked, 'Well, who would have thought that, Eva!' with a sly grin on her face. 'You might actually be good at it... not! 'I ignored her comment.

A couple of days later, Peg, the headmistress had made her decision. It was again announced in assembly. She began addressing the assembly by saying:

'This is an unusual request which has been put to me by the headmaster. I have given this request serious thought and have decided, rather cautiously, to give my permission for girl pupils, above the age of fourteen, to be included if they so wish, to join the caving and potholing group on their outings. This I do, as long as their parents give written permission to the school and the girls undertake detailed instructions, as required, to make them proficient in the sport. It can be a very dangerous pastime. I have not come to this decision lightly and any girl showing stupidity, will be stopped from participating. I hope I make myself clear!'

That was it, Rebecca thought, *Job done!*

CHAPTER 22

The list on the notice board soon filled up with names; mostly boys' names, but there were eight girls' names up there too including Bernie, me, Belinda Rudd, and Charlotte Jackson, who was in the year below us; a quiet girl, but Rebecca got on well with her. And of course, Rebecca's name was there too.

They would all stay on Friday after school for the initial talk by Mr Grey and the instructor who was also head boy, Barry Harker. All the girls really looked forward to it.

There was netball practice on the Thursday after school to get ready for the Saturday match but all fell into insignificance compared to the new challenge on the agenda.

The first part of the lesson was introductory; we were learning all about reliability on each other and later were introduced to all the equipment needed for descents into crevices and caves. There was so much equipment needed: several ropes, helmets with a headlamp, harnesses and clips called carabiners which are used to attach anchors and ropes. Someone must also have ladders.

We all had to wear protective boots and proper warm clothing as it could become very cold in the caves so far below ground. We were also told it could be very wet and we must be prepared to wade and maybe sometimes swim along the rivers inside the caves. I was very apprehensive hearing all this and knew this activity was not for me. I didn't want to appear negative but I would need everything I could muster to actually descend a rope and be a capable part of this group.

So, I kept quiet!

We had to be able to walk, climb, abseil, crawl and swim in order to explore a cave, as it had many different features and some features were referred to as rooms. It would be challenging and very demanding. I could see Mr Grey and Barry were painting a very difficult picture for the group, probably trying to put us off. They had certainly succeeded with me; I wasn't in the least looking forward to the practice we had to do before the real event.

If we succeeded and passed all the practical tests, we would feel a great sense of achievement. These exercises would also be part of team-building ready for outings for real.

There were a few minutes given to a short practice. We each paired up with one person. I was with Charlotte, and Bernie with Rebecca made a pair. We attached the harnesses to each other and were shown how to attached the carabiners to the ropes. It was all very serious; no one was mucking about which usually happened. We were told how imperative it was that we could rely on each other as it was a serious business, not for the faint-hearted.

At the end of our first instruction, we had to prove to Mr Grey and Barry that we were fit enough and if we were not, to get fit and improve our upper body strength. So, they sprang it on us; we all had to shin up the ropes which hung from the ceiling in the main hall.

There was a mad rush, except for me, to get from the double

classrooms, to the assembly hall, which was also used as the sports hall.

Rebecca eagerly awaited her turn as Eddie held the bottom of the ropes for her. She shinned up the rope like a monkey and started doing somersaults at the top, showing off as usual, I thought. She ascended even quicker and jumped onto the floor as if she was an Olympic gymnast throwing her arms in the air. The group applauded. She was such a show-off!

I just about managed to climb the blessed rope, well, I nearly reached the top but it took me a long time before I descended clumsily to the floor, rubbing my sore hands due to the friction with the ropes. Nothing was said by Barry or Mr Grey but I could tell they weren't impressed. Rebecca commented as I hit the floor, 'Well Eva you'll need to do better than that for anyone to rely on you!'

What a bitch! I felt so embarrassed and I knew I was flushed.

There she goes again, I thought, *always trying to put someone down, usually me, because she always got away with it.*

I said my goodnight to Phillip before we caught the bus back to Moonacre. This bus journey was a treat, we usually had to walk.

Our dinner was keeping warm. We were all starving hungry and tucked into one of Miss Livingstone's homemade meat and potato pies with cabbage and mash. What would we all do without Miss Livingstone's great dinners? We all looked forward to them each day as school dinners were not good. Everyone thought that. She was such a nice lady and we could all have a laugh with her and she gave back as much as we gave to her, but all in fun.

In the dorm that night again, the chat before sleep was about what we had learnt in the talk. It was mostly Bernie and Rebecca as Charlotte was still in another dormitory and Belinda had moved to the senior girls' boarding house. I pretended I was asleep, but I could hear them whispering to each other and it wouldn't have taken a genius to know they were talking about me. I was getting used to this sort of bullying, as I called it; always the weaker person Rebecca picked on, never anyone her senior.

She always sucked up to them and of course, they thought she was marvellous.

They just didn't know her!

CHAPTER 23

It was disappointing that the girls lost their netball game against Queen Elizabeth Grammar School. The opponents' team was very good and nearly always won their fixtures. Not to worry though, there was always the hockey fixture which was more competitive. I wasn't a member of either of the teams but I went as a spectator to support the school.

We always had lunch down at school on a Saturday and afterwards went on one of our weekend walks. I had arranged to meet Phillip again at Big Stone, a huge stone, set amongst the moorland scenery, quite majestic and boy, could the wind soar and blow around the rock, making you wobble if you were unsteady on your feet. We loved to sit on the top and just talk, whatever the weather and sometimes talked about the future. It was Phillip who always made me feel braver than I was. He told me I must not let her, meaning Rebecca, ever show she was getting the better of me and with regards to the caving and potholing he would make sure I was fit and strong enough to take on the challenge.

'We will show all of them, Eva, once you put your mind to it and gain some confidence, you will be just as good as all of them,' Phillip stated with passion in his voice. How could I possibly refute his words, I would try my hardest to pass the instruction test. I wouldn't ever have put this activity on my bucket list but with Phillip's support I would try my damnedest to make it work.

Rebecca was meeting Eddie up in the village, they were going to Mrs Big Nose's Cafe to have some scones with jam which were freshly baked.

Bernie was still with Pete and they were to join them. Then, they were going for a walk to Shaky Bridge. The boys hadn't been there and it would be the first time she had returned since Tony had died.

It was quite damp as the rain had swollen the River When and the streams, which flowed down into the big river, ran like torrents. They had fun jumping over them at the widest point possible, which inevitably caused wet clothes and extremely wet feet. Pushing each other in the streams was the funniest and they all belly laughed especially when one of them fell in proper. The streams and the river always won.

All soaking wet through, they made their way back. There was no film down at school that evening so there was no rush to get ready to go out again. After the girls' dinner and supper, they settled down to watch the Saturday film on the television in Carr Hall, the drawing room. Most of them kept quiet during the film but there was always one of them who wanted to talk through it.

The younger ones were not allowed to watch the nine o'clock film as it was lights out for them at eight o'clock. The older girls had this privilege on a Saturday night. They could also have their supper during the film and eat it from a tray on their knees, followed by hot chocolate or another milky drink.

It was a funny film called *Doctor in the House*, an old one from the 1950s, but it was funny and light-hearted to go to bed on. Fortunately, it was easy to follow so no interruptions, other than laughter.

Sleep followed, no midnight wanderings this Saturday night.

Walking in crocodile formation as usual down to church, a ritual each Sunday morning, except when it was evensong, but it was still in crocodile, there were always shouts by prefects of 'Hurry up, you lot', 'Stop dawdling' and 'Keep up, otherwise we will be late'.

At least the weather was fine this morning so the walk was enjoyable.

Eddie and Rebecca chatted outside church after the morning service, but were soon moved along by the duty housemaster, Mr Jones, a short, plump man who was always dishing out corporal punishments to the boys, should they be caught breaking any rules or regulations.

He taught geography and Rebecca was always mimicking him, the way he glided through the corridors when he walked, with his black gown flowing behind him, as if the poor gown dared not do anything else! He grunted and mumbled at the boys under his breath and Rebecca mimicked this.

I have to say I thought it was quite funny, she could be a good laugh, some of the time.

She parted from Eddie, walking behind Mr Jones, again mimicking the way he walked. Eddie laughed.

We couldn't meet the boys this afternoon because of the fire practice at Moonacre; a sight to behold I must say. The dorm captain had to lower the rope ladders out of each dormitory window and, with bottoms in the air, we intrepidly descended the unstable contraption to the ground, into the front garden of Moonacre. The sound of cars passing by, hooting their horns, was not an unusual occurrence.

I often thought that surely there must be another way, we were meant to be ladies, (when it suited us, I suppose) and this action was certainly not ladylike with bums up in the air. We usually all had a laugh at the situation and waved back at the passing motorists, much to Matron's disgust. She would utter, 'You're like girls from Piccadilly, and you know what they are!'

Of course, we didn't know what she meant but still thought it was funny.

Another start to the week. It would be the Easter holidays soon but we had all decided we wanted to have a little practice out on the moors. We had had a few introductory lectures and plenty of practising with the harnesses and ropes and we felt it was time to put our learning into a practical experience.

Mr Grey said he was going to arrange a walk near Ingelton where there were caves suitable for beginners and potholes to explore, so we could get the feel of what it would be like to be underground a little way.

It had to be a Saturday, when there were no netball and hockey fixtures so Mr Grey arranged this accordingly.

We rose early on the Saturday morning and devoured our breakfast, eating it before all the other girls came down. We collected our packed lunches from the kitchen, which included spam and lettuce sandwiches, a Blue Riband wafer biscuit and two Rich Tea biscuits. There was always a Rich Tea biscuit included in a picnic usually with a piece of lettuce shoved between two. On some picnic outings, we had to form a queue just to be given the biscuits by Matron. It was so funny and we laughed a lot at this.

Our thermos flasks came in handy; they were filled with tea to warm us up if need be. It was the first time I had used mine. I really wasn't looking forward to this outing. The only good thing about the morning, it was fine and clear and I think the sun was actually going to shine.

The hired coach collected us from Moonacre and the boys were already on the coach. Our destination was to be Clapham Village. We could start from the car park there and wend our way on the tarmac minor road to the gravel, stony and grass tracks, which would lead us to the entrance shaft of a large, well-explored, pothole named Gaping Gill. It was very well known – even I had heard of Gaping Gill – but never in a million years did I think I would be part of a group to descend into its bowels.

There were some steep inclines and declines to get to it and it took us going on three hours to reach the entrance. We were informed that Gaping Gill was a natural cave about nine-ty-eight metres in depth. It was a landmark on the southern slopes of Ingleborough, a yawning abyss, engulfing Britain's highest unbroken waterfall, Fell Beck, which flows into its chamber, Fortunately, this day, a caving club had provided a winch from the entrance of the pot to its chamber floor. Mr Grey had arranged it, as it was only our first time experiencing a pothole and he thought it may be a safer and more pleasant option for us.

We were all kitted out ready for the descent in the winch. Head torches were lit and one by one we descended into the limestone rock pot. The rock was very wet and it was extremely dark. The only sounds which echoed throughout were the metal scraping of the winch and the dripping of the water flowing down the surface of the rocks.

Barry Harker, the head boy, was at the bottom on the cave floor to assist us out of the winch. It was dark, cold and damp. We were told to stay in position until the last one of us had descended. I was glad of my warm clothing, I had never been anywhere so cold, damp and gloomy and wondered why this activity attracted so many.

Rebecca arrived followed by Eddie. She seemed to be enjoying the activity and the two of them huddled together to keep warm whilst we were all standing about.

Once we were all down on the cave floor, we were told we would be walking a short way along the passages. We would be privy to the hidden world of stalagmites and stalactites and maybe have to dodge the odd bat along the way. We may, at some stage, but maybe not this time, have to negotiate underground rivers and thunderous waterfalls.

More experienced cavers would travel a long way through difficult tunnels, terrain and crevices to reach another exit point within this pothole but that was not for beginners as we were. I could see how the water could do extraordinary things to the rocks, sculpting them into weird shapes where the stone took on an effect of a frozen chocolate fountain. And the stalagmites and stalactites were amazing; some thick forms and some more delicate pieces hanging down from the roof of the caves, quite beautiful; a whole different world.

After a walk of about twenty minutes, we had to retrace our steps. Mr Grey led the way and Barry brought up the rear. We were slowly winched back up to the top. I was one of the first and elated as the light from the daytime sky shone down, enticing me to the top. I knew I was near the top when I could see the green foliage; grasses and ferns which clung to the rocks at the entrance to the pot.

That was me happy; the walk back to the coach didn't worry me. I felt tired but I realised I had accomplished something very real and I was so pleased with myself.

As each one of us reached the top, an urgent hot drink was needed. We all drank our hot tea from the thermos flasks we had brought with us.

I was shivering and couldn't wait to set off back down the mountain to the lower slopes to get the blood circulating through my body once again.

It was a good sight when we got to the car park, to actually see something man-made! Phillip laughed at my comment and said, 'Don't worry Eva, we will make a caver out of you yet.'

We sat together on the coach back to Moonacre and had a cuddle, more to keep us warm than anything else.

Of course, Rebecca was lording it on the back seat, discussing how easy she felt it all was and maybe next time instead of the winch, she would like to abseil down to the cavern floor herself. Eddie was with her and eventually they were quiet.

Mr Grey was sitting at the front of the coach so couldn't see them kissing and cuddling on the back seat of the coach. It reminded me of the song, 'Seven Little Girls Sitting in the Back Seat'. We sometimes used to sing that song when we were on the bus going on school outings or to away matches.

The back seat of the coach went very quiet.

CHAPTER 24

In assembly the following Monday morning, Joss covered the weekend's sporting events and notices regarding the activities of the forthcoming week. There were hockey and netball practices; the drama group were to meet, they were rehearsing for Shakespeare's 'Twelfth Night', which was to be performed prior to the end of the term.

He then congratulated all the cavers on their accomplishment of the first successful descent into Gaping Gill pot; especially the girls, who had all done tremendously well. He said he was pleased with this progress and maybe in the future we would have a champion girl from Brantham, as a very famous successful potholer.

That's me, Rebecca secretly thought and she turned her head to seek out Eddie on the other side of the assembly hall.

As the days lengthened, it gave the cavers the opportunity to walk on the lower slopes near Ingelton and practise their skills in the potholes in that area. It was not a time-consuming walk to reach the caves from school especially if the last two lessons were double games and the group could set off earlier before school had ended.

Some of the entrances to these caves were very small spaces and involved climbing, squeezing, and squirming your way into openings in the earth's rocks to discover many fascinating large and beautiful caverns under the surface. Rebecca had no fear, she seemed to adapt herself easily to the agility needed to enter these very small spaces and flatten her body in order to shin along the surfaces using her feet, knees, and elbows.

Wherever she was, Eddie was always close behind her. They seem to have taken to the sport and were in sync with each other. It also appeared to me that Rebecca was becoming more accomplished at caving than Eddie was, especially when she dictated instructions to him and he adhered to them. Phillip and I didn't always go on these outings but we tried to do some of them; really in order to see each other, especially as the days were lengthening and we could spend more time together.

I could tell Mr Grey always kept a special eye on me as he knew I was more of a liability than the rest of them. I wasn't as agile and strong but I was getting there, Phillip saw to that. He would give me exercises to do: squats and push-ups which I found difficult but I still did them religiously each day and slowly my upper body strength improved.

The Easter holidays arrived and we all went off for a three-week holiday, leaving potholing where it belonged, up there on the Yorkshire moors and dales.

I didn't live too far away from Brantham and my elder brother, who was also at the school, drove me home. Phillip and I had planned to see each other at some stage in the holidays but there was nothing rigidly fixed so we would see what happened. Rebecca said her goodbyes to Eddie outside the main school gates and they hoped to meet up at his house in

Blackpool during the long break, but Rebecca knew she had to make the long train journey to Cornwall, so again nothing was determined.

She ran across the bridge over the River When to the pub car park where her friend's father patiently waited for the two girls to ferry them home. It had landed on this kind gentleman to do this each time the girls needed collecting from school and also the return journey.

Grandma and Grandpa were pleased to see Rebecca and told her they had booked her train journey to Cornwall in two days' time. Grandma said she would have all her laundry washed and ironed before she left and her school uniform would be laundered on her return, ready for the start of the new term.

Grandma Ellershaw and Uncle Tony visited the following day and were eager to hear all the stories Rebecca had. She told them how successful she was at caving and they shared their thoughts that it was far too dangerous for her to be involved in. She brushed their comments aside and stated it was perfectly safe as it was fully supervised and she knew the dangers, but she was good at it.

The train for Cornwall left Leeds Central Station at twelve midnight. It was the night sleeper directly down to Penzance. Grandma had booked Rebecca into a sleeping compartment. The compartment was very small consisting of bunk beds with two shelves at the side of them and a small wash hand basin in the corner. The sleeping compartments were attended by a guard in uniform, who informed Rebecca he would knock on the door about fifteen minutes before they reached their destination, which would give her time to wash and dress. Her mother would collect her from the station at Redruth, which was only a few stops from the end of the line.

She felt very grown up, as this was the first long journey on a train by herself, ever. She shared the compartment with a nice lady who was also travelling alone and she was going to occupy the lower bunk. This worked out very well and they got into an interesting conversation about the lady's family. In turn, Rebecca told her about all her caving exploits, exaggerating her skills, nevertheless, before they were both lulled away to sleep by the rocking of the train as it sped into the darkness on its long journey south.

At dawn, a light breakfast was served by the guard, of tea and toast in the sleeping compartment. Rebecca had slept very well and became excited at the thought of seeing her mum and Rufus. She also wondered what the new house was like. She had never visited this part of Cornwall before.

The train pulled into the small station at Redruth at about eight o'clock and the commuters were all waiting on the opposite platform for a train to take them on their usual daily journey north. Rebecca enjoyed travelling by train and the thought passed through her mind that maybe she would be commuting when she was older and perhaps had a job in the City.

Dragging her case off the train and onto the platform she hurried up the steps and over the bridge which crossed the railway lines and down the other side. There they were, Mum and Rufus waiting for her. How she had missed them both. They hugged each other and Rufus went crazy, circling her and his tail also making circling motions; if he could have smiled and laughed, he would have done. They never stopped talking on the way back to the new house.

Her mum was driving a new Land Rover, a blue one, which she used for her milk round. She explained that Robert had a pickup truck for his milk round and it appeared to Rebecca that life here was good for them. She was pleased her mum seemed happy, although she said the work was challenging as the milk crates were heavy to lift, but she was getting used to it.

It was about twelve miles to the new house, which turned out to be a small bungalow just outside a village called Mawgan. It was brand new. There were three bedrooms, lounge and a kitchen and an Aga cooker which heated all the hot water and kept the house warm as it was on all the time. Robert was due home soon, her mum said. He was out collecting the milk round money in order for him to keep his books up to date and so he could submit them to the accountant very soon. *That's posh; having an accountant*, Rebecca thought.

Rebecca was happy, she had her own bedroom at the bungalow which was in the back and, although she had no view of the sea, there was a great view over the countryside and fields. The field directly behind the bungalow housed a pony which belonged to the farm nearby and there was also a donkey called Rupert; a new member of the Tay family. Robert had given it a home as the previous owner could no longer look after it. The man had become too old and had to sell his property and the field where Rupert lived.

Rebecca was overjoyed on seeing Rupert and during the two weeks she was on holiday she walked often with him on the end of a rope down the tracks and lanes near to the bungalow. She also brushed and pampered him and always made sure she put him in his small stone-built stable for his night's sleep. Rupert and Rebecca became great chums. She would be sad to leave him. Robert told her he was planning to have a small two- seater carriage made, so Rupert could pull it along into the village to collect the shopping. She was elated with this idea and of course, it gave the two of them something pleasant to talk about.

The position of the bungalow wasn't to everyone's taste. It was situated on the edge of the airfield of Royal Naval Air Station Culdrose. For those of us who enjoy watching helicopters passing our front door it was an ideal spot, but it could be very noisy. At the end of the cul-de-sac, was the public viewing enclosure for the airfield and this could get very busy, with enthusiasts gazing and taking photographs of the Sea King helicopters taking off and landing.

It wasn't all a holiday for Rebecca. Whilst she was there, Robert insisted she helped her mum on the milk round, which meant her rising early each morning, delivering the milk to the customers doorsteps and all before eight o'clock. Rebecca could appreciate how her mum was always tired when she arrived home at about lunch time each day after the early morning start. She had always intended to help her mum and took umbrage at Robert trying to tell her what to do. She had managed quite well without him interfering in her life and wasn't going to start adhering to all his rules and regulations again. *Let him drone on*, Rebecca thought, *there will be other ways I can eventually sort him out.*

This comforted her: 'Where there's a will, there's a way, another of grandma's sayings.

Each day was a struggle, to get up, but it was always later in the day Rebecca felt exhausted. She didn't really feel like being sociable in the evening because she was so tired. Her mum noticed this and decided to let her have the Saturday morning off dairy duties, much to her delight, and had arranged for Rebecca to go to the local camp dance on the navy base with another girl. Marian had become friends with the girl's mother and Rebecca was invited to tag along with her daughter, Natasha, and her friends.

This news delighted her and immediately she started to plan what she was going to wear. It just had to be the pale blue crêpe dress with the pearl buttons, the one her mother had made and which she wore to the school social. There would be no blue ribbon tied around her ponytail this time as she had had her hair cut very short to be in trend with her mod friends.

There were six of them attending the camp dance. They were all Natasha's friends. Rebecca had met Natasha earlier in the week and they seemed to get on very well. The six of them met up at Natasha's and Rebecca was eager to know all about the dances and who would be there.

The dances were held on a Saturday night each month and several of the local girls attended. It was like a honey pot for the local girls. They all received so much attention from the young sailors, who hadn't always seen much female company. Many of the sailors worked on the camp as mechanics and in other trades, but some of the others returned from their postings at sea. So female company was enjoyed by the young men. There was many a romance that blossomed after one of these camp dances. The music was provided by a local group who performed songs by The Beatles, The Searchers and The Fortunes and also, to Rebecca's delight, an Ike and Tina Turner song.

The girls were all dancing in a group with about five boys, all twisting the night away when one boy sidled up alongside Rebecca. He wasn't dancing, just standing annoyingly in front of her staring; in fact, he became quite annoying. She moved away around the other side of the ring, but he followed and again stood in front of her.

'What's your problem?' Rebecca shouted at him. The band was very loud and it was difficult to talk quietly. 'You're stopping me from dancing. Why don't you dance instead of just standing there?' she continued.

He didn't answer her; just placed himself in front of her again and stared.

The other girls started to giggle and that made Rebecca giggle and they then all walked over to a table serving soft drinks, to quench their thirst.

There was no alcohol being served at the dance, but it would appear some of the boys had their own stash of drink, which had been consumed earlier. It was noticed and brought to Rebecca's attention that the same boy was still staring at her across the room. He hadn't taken his eyes off her.

'Think you've pulled,' the girls joked and Rebecca rebuffed them.

'He's not my type,' she answered. 'Besides, I have a boyfriend at school who I am going steady with.' She was secretly flattered and was exuberant at all the attention. The more she laughed and danced the more interested the boy seemed to be and eventually he made his way over to the dance floor. He stood in front of her again and moved slowly backwards and forwards and started to dance, still not saying a word.

He looked quite a cool dancer, especially when he spun around and faced her again. She stopped dancing and held out her hands as if to say 'What do you want?'

He whispered in her ear, 'I want to dance with you, without all these hangers-on around you.' He put his arm around her waist and they moved together in time to the music. It was a slow dance and he breathed heavily in her ear.

This is weird, she thought, but in a strange way she was intrigued by his approach and went with the status quo. He wasn't a bad looking boy, about twenty years old and a good head height above her. He had very piercing dark eyes and she couldn't tell what colour they were as the hall was too dark. He sounded as if he was from London. She liked his voice and he called her 'babe'. No one had ever called her that before and she liked it.

He kept pulling her closer to him and started to rub his lips over her neck and suck her ear lobe. This went on throughout the dance. When the dance ended, he said, 'I'll see you around, babe,' and walked away to a group of his friends.

She didn't dance with him again and left the building with the other girls but, as she walked down the block outside, she heard a whistle.

Turning, there was the lad again, standing at the corner of a residential block.

'I'll phone you,' he shouted.

'You haven't my number, have you? So how are you going to do that?'

'You're going to give it to me now,' he said.

Cheek, Rebecca thought, *he is so self-assured*, so she just walked on. It wasn't long before he caught up with her at the main entrance to the camp.

'Before you go, give me your number,' he said, without a please or a thank you. 'I like you and want to meet up again.'

'You don't even know my name or anything about me,' Rebecca snapped back.

'That's why I want your number,' he said with a soft smile on his face.

'Ok, phone me tomorrow, without drink in you, whatever your name is!' She wrote her number down on a piece of paper with her eyebrow pencil and left.

'My name's Frankie,' he shouted after her.

CHAPTER 25

*F*rankie, she thought, *well, we'll see if he's as good as his word, probably the drink talking. I'm sure, he had a few tots of rum before he came to the dance.* She still had another week in Cornwall so plenty of time to see if he lived up to his words.

She didn't have to wait long as that Sunday evening after seven the phone rang. It was always cheaper to phone after seven which Rebecca knew because she always phoned her mum on a Sunday night and got it cheaper after seven. Robert got to the telephone first and was somewhat cautious when he heard an unfamiliar voice on the other end. *That was a pity* thought Rebecca. She almost knew by Robert's demeanour and by how he thrust the phone in her hand that he wasn't best pleased.

They arranged to see each other the following Tuesday night, at a local church hall. There was to be the Jug and Bottle Band from the camp performing in the hall and would she like to go. She didn't know what a jug and bottle band was and didn't really care, but going out with Frankie might be interesting and it would be something to look forward to, after a couple of early mornings delivering milk.

She kept quiet about her date and decided she would only tell her mum on the Tuesday when they were out on the milk round. Robert was inquisitive as to the strange caller on the phone but all Rebecca would say was that he was a friend. She could sense the bad atmosphere at a hundred yards when he was in the room and with a quip he stated:

'Don't you be bringing any trouble to this house, do you hear?'

Tuesday arrived soon enough and she was collected at the end of the road by Frankie and the other band members.

The band had an old van which was painted in psychedelic colours with writing along the panels both inside and out. They would travel to all the local gigs in the van as it housed all their musical equipment... I say that loosely. They didn't take themselves too seriously, always laughing and joking with each other, referring to themselves as The Bug and Jottle Band.

There was a washboard with metal caps for the players' fingers, an old tea chest, with a piece of string attached and the other end attached to a broom handle which served as a bass. There was another band member, who blew into the hole of a flat ceramic bottle whilst he used his foot to hit the drum, and another band member, played the spoons.

The back of the van was also kitted out with a large mattress so all the members of the band could travel together in comfort. Frankie seemed to be the organiser; he played a guitar which he carried slung over his shoulder. Rebecca was so pleased he had invited her along and she seemed to be accepted by the rest of the band.

The gig was not in the church hall as originally planned, the organisers had commandeered the farmer's barn which was ideally packed full of giant bales of hay, perfect for the band

and plenty of seating for the rest of the revellers. There were strings of lights hanging all around the walls of the barn and flashing lights which danced in time to the music, played.

The Bug and Jottle Band played their hoedown repertoire and everyone seemed to love the authenticity of this crazy band who were all dressed to resemble scarecrows. They wore straw hats, bibs and braces, and there was no orifice without a piece of straw coming out of it. They did look the part and everyone seemed to love them. They even got another booking for the following week at another country fair.

Frankie was great on the guitar and he held the band together. They all sang and took it in turns to join in the country dancing with the crowd.

The evening ended with Rebecca and the rest of the band lounging around on the hay bales, consuming the bottled beer which was provided free for the band, as payment for the gig.

She actually wasn't late home that evening. The band dropped her off on the camp public viewing enclosure, a few yards away from her front door. Her parents must have heard them arrive back, as the music was blaring out from the van into the quiet, stillness of the countryside.

It was unlikely Rebecca would see Frankie again as she had to return to school the following week and had to return to Grandma's prior to this.

She had enjoyed the evening and hadn't stopped laughing. She liked Frankie; he was so light-hearted as were the other band members, who were all sailors as well. Frankie and she had exchanged addresses. He said he would write to her when she was back at school and even suggested he could visit her when he was next on leave. Rebecca agreed to this although she realised she was going to have some juggling moments, what with Geoff, Eddie and now Frankie, who all wanted to see her; but she hoped, not all at once.

However, she wasn't going to worry about it, it would all sort itself out; all in good time.

Robert expressed his opinion about a liaison with a sailor boy saying, in reference to Frankie, 'Don't get involved there, Rebecca; they have girls all over the place, in every port. Then they go to sea and the wives are left alone for months on end. Do you want that sort of life for yourself? You would be better concentrating on your studies and getting a good job, never mind the sailor boys.'

She wasn't going to bite back, that's probably what he wanted, but she would remember his words, yet again.

Before she left Cornwall, she decided to give her mother a treat and a rest from the morning milk round. Her mother had taught her well and she knew all the houses where milk must be delivered. She was just missing a driver. This hurdle was overcome, as a friend and assistant on Robert's round came to the rescue. It would give her mum a chance to rest, as she and Robert were attending a dinner dance that evening.

Mum had a lovely cocktail dress; knee-length was all the fashion. She had made it herself. Robert was to wear his evening suit with his dress shirt. It was the annual Rotary Club's dinner and dance; Robert had joined the association when they moved to Cornwall. It was to be held in a big hotel, over towards Newquay.

There was to be a four-course dinner, followed by speeches and dancing until about midnight, then breakfast would be served before carriages at two o'clock in the morning. She wanted her mum to have a lovely evening out and not be tired as she had looked exhausted on some days and that worried Rebecca.

Her mum looked beautiful in her new dress. It was emerald green, with sparkly stones and sequins in abundance around the neckline. She had her hair highlighted and the top was held in place with a diamond clip, a present from Robert when they married.

There was also ironing to do that afternoon and Rebecca set to and helped her mum with this chore. Happily, there was Robert's dress shirt to iron, which came out yearly for this sort of occasion. It was always washed and put away unironed until the next occasion. The iron needed to be very hot for the creased collar. It was Marian's heavy dressmaking iron. It was a mystery to Marian as to why chewing gum had caught on the hot iron and hence had spread onto the shirt collar as Rebecca ironed away. It was a mess and couldn't be worn. It was also far too late to buy another shirt as the shops were closed and they were due to leave very shortly.

Robert was beside himself, yelling at Rebecca, accusing her of deliberately sabotaging the shirt. He was livid, uttering words, to the effect: the sooner you leave here, girl, the better it will all be for all of us.

Once again, her mum was between the devil and the deep blue sea, not knowing which way to turn. It was such a pity; Marian was so looking forward to this special occasion. But there was nothing more to be done. Robert wore a plain white shirt under his evening suit; not ideal but it was his only option.

'Have a nice evening,' Rebecca remarked as they walked out of the door. She chewed on the rest of the Wrigley's spearmint gum, but kept the wrapper.

CHAPTER 26

Rebecca met Frankie the following day after the milk round. Her mum had another day off, which she thoroughly deserved. They met in the local village cafe which wasn't too far for Rebecca to walk. Again, he made her laugh and she confided in him about her step-dad's dress shirt collar. They both roared with laughter. She had already told him about how Robert had hit her and how he was always causing her a problem so he thought the incident very funny and believed he deserved all he got.

She joined him in smoking the Royal Navy cigarettes from the white box with RN emblazoned in navy blue across the middle of it.

Frankie explained they could buy them cheaply as it was the Royal Navy's own brand. He joked, that sometimes you might get a lump of wood in the middle of the tobacco; they were so cheap! He gave her a packet to remind her of him and for her to smoke on the journey back to Lancashire. They arranged to write to each other and he was insistent about wanting to visit her on his next leave suggesting that maybe they could have a few days' holiday in Blackpool as he had never been there before, or seen the Blackpool illuminations.

It was nice, Rebecca thought, getting to know Frankie and she was warming to him. She would look forward to his letters and see what transpired. She liked the fact that Frankie was cool about their relationship and not gushing all over her. He was a challenge!

The following day was hot. Only a couple more days to lie in the sunshine and get a little bit of a tan before the long train journey home.

She decided after the milk round she would change into her bikini and sprawl out on the sun lounger in the garden, soaking up the sun's rays for the whole afternoon.

Inevitably, Rebecca fell sound asleep. She was tired; the early mornings had also taken their toll on her and she was exhausted. The sun was hot that afternoon, not a cloud in the sky and, although she had applied suntan lotion, she had mistakenly not applied enough. She awoke, but not by the sun burning her, although she was as red as a lobster, but by the dark shadow of Robert Tay standing over her blocking the sun from her body. His face was raging as he grabbed hold of her left arm and pulled her off the lounger onto the grass, tipping the sunbed up as she fell.

He grabbed her arm again and twisted it so as to see the tattoo emblazoned in the crook of her arm. She had forgotten to cover it up and was taken unaware as Robert seethed over the disgusting tattoo. He was livid and lashed out at her again with Rufus's dog chain on her bare, red skin, like a man possessed, causing red slash marks over her arms and some on her chest.

'Get out of my sight and house, you dirty trollop,' Robert shouted, 'or I'll whip you again. I never want to set eyes on you again.'

The pain for Rebecca was excruciating, coupled with the sunburn as well. She ran into the house and immediately packed her clothes into the holdall and weekender case. Her mum hadn't witnessed the cruelty by Robert Tay, she only heard the commotion and immediately went to her daughter's aid. She bathed and dressed her wounds and rocked her in her arms until Rebecca fell asleep.

In Marian's mind this was also the final straw that broke the camel's back. She made her mind up that this man was cruel and unforgiving and she would find her own way out of this relationship in the coming months, no matter what!

No one would ever beat her daughter and draw blood again. Marian looked at the tattoo Rebecca had been hiding, she slowly stroked her daughter's wound and put it to her lips and kissed it. Her love was unconditional.

Mum took her to the station for the train back to Lancashire, her tears unhidden from Rebecca. Uncle John, cousin Betty's dad, was to collect her and drive her back to Grandma's.

It was a long journey back, but she had the company of a few people sitting at the same table in the carriage to chat to, so that helped break the monotony. She also managed to rest and sleep on the train. She had taken painkillers which her mum had given her to help with the sunburn as well as the pain.

Thankfully, Uncle John and Grandma were at the station to help Rebecca with her luggage and support her home. It was lovely to have them meet her, she felt warm and loved and would never forget their help.

She didn't wish to go into details about the fight, not just at this moment in time, but let them know her wounds were painful and so was the sunburn. Grandma and Uncle John respected her wishes but as was Grandma's way she verbally cursed Robert Tay and Grandma didn't normally curse.

After a good night's sleep at Grandma's, Rebecca felt able to face the day and the three companions discussed the incident together over a large Lancashire breakfast. She felt better as she got the whole story off her chest to Grandma and Grandpa. She could see their anger and hatred for what he had done to her and they threatened to never let this matter rest until justice was done.

The following day it was decided that Rebecca should return to school. Grandma had written a letter to Matron explaining the injuries to Rebecca and how she had sustained them. It didn't make very happy reading, but the facts were laid out, no holds barred. Back at school, all the girls rushed around hugging and kissing each other. They were so pleased to see their best friends; it had been a long holiday.

I had seen Phillip in the holiday and he had also been introduced to both my parents and brothers. They all seemed to like him and I was so in love with him by this time. I did not look at another boy and just wanted to spend all my time with him. He said he felt the same way and when we were old enough and left school we would get married as soon as we could.

I didn't tell anyone of our commitment as I didn't want it to be ridiculed, especially by Rebecca, as she would have cheapened the whole thing and would have been joking and cynical.

That was Phillip's and my secret.

At the end of the summer term, our age group would leave Moonacre for good and on our return in the Autumn, we would all be juniors in Ford House, the girls' new boarding house about half a mile down the road from Moonacre, nearer the school. We were all looking forward to leaving the draughty building with the wooden floors and dark green painted walls and iron bedsteads. In Ford House, we would have divan beds and our own dressing table. The rooms in the house were small, so a maximum of four girls in each room. It was all so lovely and warm, centrally heated, and double glazing on the windows... so no draughts!

However, we had to endure this last term in Moonacre, which wasn't too bad, as the weather was now getting warmer and we were not waking up to a freezing cold dorm as we did in the winter terms.

Rebecca, to me, hadn't changed, she was still loud and we all heard about her Cornish trip and this new guy Frankie but she never did explain the injuries she received in that school holiday and just said the sunburn caused the scars. She wasn't very careful, as to who knew about Frankie. She was still with Eddie and if he found out about her new escapades, I am sure he wouldn't have been best pleased. He obviously hadn't heard as they still seemed friendly enough at the morning break when we were all waiting around the tuck shop. They were laughing and holding hands and everything seemed to be fine until Pippa Jones walked by and the moment Eddie saw her, he moved away from Rebecca.

I noticed this, but I don't think Rebecca did, she was too full of herself. Pippa walked over to Eddie and had a conversation with him, much to the disgust of Rebecca. She was livid and questioned Eddie about the conversation. Pippa, left the two of them arguing, with a smirk over her face. Eddie and Pippa, had once been an item but they broke up when he took up with Rebecca. She had never forgiven Rebecca, saying that she had stolen him away from her.

I watched on with interest. It would be a real drama if Eddie and Pippa got back together again. I didn't like feeling vengeful, it wasn't my nature, but I secretly hoped this would happen. I kept my thoughts to myself.

In class Rebecca was very quiet. She sat together with Helena as usual and with friends Lynn Barton and Rose Parker, who were both day girls.

They all seemed to put up with her and there was no discord ever between them.

It was a good job, I thought, that Pippa Jones was already living at Ford House, so Rebecca and she didn't see each other in the evenings.

Let's hope any feud they had between them would be over by the beginning of next term.

The following day at school, Eddie and Rebecca seemed to be back to normal with each other. They must have resolved their differences as they were talking normally and discussing the next outing for caving, which was to be the coming weekend.

The pot to tackle on the forthcoming weekend, or should I say, descend is known as Lost John's pot. It is named after two men who were both named John. It is told that the two men's candles had gone out whilst underground and they utterly lost their way. The pot is situated on Leck Fell, Lancashire, with three major vertical routes of entrance.

During this visit, we were to descend and visit the aqueous

Rumbling Hole inlet along the way downstream which can be easily followed for several hundred metres. We were to return via the same route until we became more efficient.

Eddie and Rebecca stayed together on the abseil down from the entrance of the pot and were bringing up the rear with Barry, the head boy, who was also with us all again. Mr Grey led from the front. He seemed very pleased with our progress and I have to say, in particular, with Rebecca as her leadership skills came to the fore. Her first-aid kit was always at the ready, should there be any minor injuries. She was always the first person to treat any injuries and I think Mr Grey and Barry were overwhelmed with her aptitude on these outings. She seemed to naturally take a leadership role, organising the group with small instructions, and generally taking the lead. So much so that she was given the task of bringing up the rear of the group with Barry. He showed her what was expected of the person at the back of the group. Eddie was not involved in this, but they still seemed amenable with each other.

I found the abseiling more difficult than I expected, although I had the support of everyone in the group, and even Rebecca was helpful and encouraging. The day over, everyone applauded as we reached the top of Lost John's pot and Rebecca got a mention for her ability and her responsibility, at such a young age.

Tea to warm us, sandwiches and yes, the statutory Rich Tea biscuits were consumed before the journey back to school. Everyone was completely worn out; the stamina needed to ascend and descend took it out of each of us. My arms and fingers were aching and my legs wouldn't stop trembling, until I had had a hot drink. I felt exhausted and fell asleep on the way back on the coach. I was again, pleased with my performance and Phillip said so as well. I told him how much I loved him and we had a special moment together. It was wonderful.

CHAPTER 27

Eddie and Rebecca seemed strained with each other, he seemed disinterested with her and she was struggling with his indifference towards her. Phillip told me, the rumour was, that Eddie had been seeing Pippa in the Easter holidays at his home. She was living in the same area with her auntie, as her parents were in the services and were posted abroad.

It all came to a head when Pippa made a comment to Rebecca on the walk back from school that day. Pippa remarked it was such a pity that she hadn't make the effort to meet Eddie in the holidays. He was at a loose end and they bumped into each other whilst walking by the sea.

So, she had spent a lot of the holiday with him, just like old times.

Rebecca was not standing for this from the senior girl, she didn't care how much more senior she was. She lunged at Pippa, who was a petite girl and shorter than Rebecca, with the heavy satchel she carried on her shoulder full of books. She swung it hard at Pippa, catching her on the side of the head, causing her to fall directly to the ground. Whilst on the ground, Rebecca continued to thump her in the body, until some of the other girls intervened and dragged Rebecca off Pippa. There was a great commotion and Pippa was definitely dazed by the satchel hitting her.

When things calmed down, Pippa was helped back to Ford House and the others all made their way back to their respective boarding houses. The fight was reported officially and Rebecca was in trouble.

The headmistress was called to Moonacre and Rebecca was interviewed by the local policeman in the presence of the headmistress.

There were no excuses for Rebecca as there were too many witnesses to the attack on Pippa. Some of the girls felt sorry for Rebecca as they knew Pippa had provoked her and, to be honest, Pippa wasn't the most popular girl in the school; she was quite aloof and strutted about with her nose in the air. She was taken to the sick bay and kept under observation all night by Matron. The doctor had given strict instructions that she must be kept quiet and still, as a head injury was always dealt with as a serious matter.

He would visit Ford House the following day to see how Pippa was.

In the meantime, Rebecca's parents were informed of the assault and were both appalled at the allegations and her actions. They both supported the school in any action they thought they should take.

Cornwall was a long way away and due to their business, they couldn't leave it to attend the school. It therefore fell to Grandma and Grandpa to sort the mess out. Luckily, Uncle John drove Grandma to the school, where she met with the headteachers and the police to see what action could be taken.

Pippa Jones didn't want any police prosecution. There was apparently no lasting damage, she would be happy with an apology.

However, the headmistress decided punishment must be given and Rebecca was to be suspended from school for two weeks and when she returned, she would be on washing-up duties until the end of term. For her, the worst of all the punishments dealt out, was she would stay a further term at Moonacre and wouldn't be moving up to Ford House with the other girls in her year, after the summer holidays. This was devastating news for her. She was okay about the other punishments dished out, but to stay behind when all her friends went to Ford was so unfair, especially when Pippa Jones got off lightly after provoking her.

She never apologised!

Rebecca did leave the school the following day, in the back seat of Uncle John's car. Grandma sat in the front seat and they drove the familiar journey across the Yorkshire moors back to Grandma's. She kept quiet, as she knew both Grandma and her uncle were not very happy with her.

The two weeks at Grandma's were spent revising for exams, she wasn't allowed to go out on her own as being suspended was a punishment. Even Grandpa agreed with this.

Occasionally they visited Grandma Ellershaw and Uncle Tony who did sympathise with her to a certain extent when they had heard the story and said she was provoked into her actions, but said she should have just walked away.

Geoff had written a letter to her at Grandma's and expressed a wish to come and see her at the school on the forthcoming exeat day, but Grandma had forbidden this as she was under punishment. Rebecca wrote back and said there wasn't to be an exeat day for her this summer term but didn't elaborate.

The two weeks went quite quickly. She wasn't looking forward to returning to school. Everything in her life felt up in the air, as if she didn't belong anywhere. She wished Harry was still there, Harry was her only really true friend. She had even lost her Eddie to that conniving bitch. She realised she had to toughen up and wouldn't be seen to be weak, even though she really didn't feel too strong.

She seemed to settle back into the routine of school and the boarding house duties. Even some of the girls congratulated her on giving Pippa Jones a good hiding… Little Miss Upstart, they called Pippa, not a popular girl! It would soon be the end of the summer term and she could put all the trouble behind her. She was resigned to the fact she would spend another term, when the autumn came at Moonacre. She wasn't happy about it, but there was not a lot she could do.

The summer holidays were upon the pupils and respectively they all left for their homes – some abroad – and Rebecca would reluctantly spend a few weeks in Cornwall. She longed to see her mum and Rufus so it was a fait accompli and she had to go. It would also be another opportunity to see Frankie as well and she was looking forward to that.

He kept his word and wrote many letters to her and she reciprocated. And they began to get to know each other this way. He wasn't around to see her for the whole six weeks of her holiday as the camp closed throughout the month of August which was when he was going home to his family, his mum's and sister's near London. But she saw Frankie on a few occasions and they spent a lot of time together when he returned to the camp after his summer holidays.

She wasn't greeted well by Robert. On her arrival, neither of them uttered a word to each other. Rebecca was to keep out of his way. Her mum sat down with her and wanted to hear about the circumstances surrounding the assault on Pippa. Rebecca was definitely a worry for Marian and she wondered how and why her daughter had these unwelcoming traits.

Water off a duck's back to Rebecca, she cared not and explained it was all in self-defence and that was all she would say about the matter.

She still treated Robert with disdain and he found it very difficult to be in the same room as her.

She wasn't up early every morning to do the milk round, just occasionally as her mother's round was now being delivered by another employee.

Rebecca was told the crates were too heavy for Marian to lift and she had a small problem with her back so needed more rest. Rebecca questioned her mum about the problem. Her mum just said she had a little tear in the muscles and needed the rest. Happy with this explanation Rebecca continued her holiday.

She saw Frankie on numerous occasions. They spent a lot of time together even though he had to work; his shift always finished at about four o'clock, which gave them plenty of time to visit places and spend time on the beaches of Cornwall. She also went in the van with the band. They were performing in the open-air theatre near to Land's End. It was a magical place high on the rocks overlooking the turquoise waters of the Atlantic Ocean. The seats were all stone, covered in grass, and in rows towering above the stage, high above the sea. It was a stunning view and one of Rebecca's very favourite places.

The summer was good and there were no conflicts to talk of between her and Robert. In fact, she was hardly in his presence. It seemed as if he had washed his hands of her. She spent time with her mum, just the two of them. They had their shopping trips and lunches out, consuming copious amounts of crab sandwiches and Cornish cream teas on these trips. Once a waitress told her off because Rebecca was putting the cream on the scone first, followed by the jam. That was the wrong way round in Cornwall; that was the Devon way. It was always jam first then cream on top. They laughed together about this and her mum said not to worry as it all tasted the same anyway.

The holiday went all too quickly and she was soon travelling back on the train, saying farewell to the Cornish beaches, cream teas, Frankie, her mum, and Rufus She reflected the holiday was a happy time and good to remember, especially before returning to school, just nothing to look forward to the coming Autumn term.

CHAPTER 28

It was strange arriving back at Moonacre; all the girls in her year were starting their new term at Ford House. There was only Charlotte Jackson she was friendly with and she joined Rebecca in the senior dormitory. The two girls got on very well; Charlotte was quieter than Rebecca, that's probably why. No one mentioned the trouble Rebecca had had with Pippa Jones and Eddie played it very cool with her during the break times at school.

As the days went on it was evident the friendship between Rebecca and Eddie had ceased to exist. He was spending his break times with Pippa and her friends. Rebecca seemed very unhappy and all the fun she used to have had drained away from her.

I was surprised. I had never seen this side of her. Sometimes I almost felt sorry for her, but then memories came flooding back of how argumentative and unkind she could be. She was certainly getting a taste of her own medicine now.

She continued to write her long letters to Frankie and he always replied; this closeness helped her, I think. Geoff, her old boyfriend, also was still in touch. He seemed kind and was eager to come to the school and take her out for exeat day. Grandma had given written permission and once again Geoff drove to the school, accompanied by his interfering mother.

I think Rebecca felt comforted with Geoff and his family still in her life, as just recently, things hadn't been too happy for her.

About a week or so after the day out with Geoff, Rebecca was asked to go to Matron's quarters. Miss Carter, the housemistress, was also present when Rebecca walked into the cosy, warm sitting room. The two matriarchs sat there with very serious faces. Rebecca wondered what she had done now to be summoned to Matron's quarters. It was a Friday evening just prior to prep time when Rebecca was given the very sad news.

Her head started to spin and she couldn't properly equate what she was hearing from Miss Carter. Matron just sat there and lowered her head. Marian was very ill; she had deteriorated since being taken into hospital all within a few days. Rebecca was unaware of anything wrong with her mum; the family had thought it better not to involve her as they thought things would improve and Rebecca would be none the wiser. The apparent small operation that Marian went into hospital for, had revealed more sinister findings and although the repair was done, they found cancerous growths in her liver and pancreas which were inoperable and she was given only a few weeks to live.

Rebecca must go to Cornwall immediately to spend her last few days by her mum's side.

It was a difficult few weeks for Rebecca to see her mum so ill and feeling totally helpless. All she could do was talk to her and make her as comfortable as possible. She slept by her mum, some nights crying herself to sleep. She knew the inevitable was going to happen very soon but must try to be strong for

Grandpa and Grandma, losing their only daughter.

It was a Saturday afternoon when Marian passed away, Rebecca was at her bedside, holding her frail hand. The person who meant everything to her had now gone. She felt totally alone, except for the constant companionship of Rufus. He sat with her by the bed most of the time and he was of great comfort. She decided, when she left Cornwall for good, Rufus would come too.

Grandpa was the rock for Grandma and Rebecca. She could always rely on Grandpa, ever since she was a little girl; he was the father she had never had. The three of them made all the funeral arrangements together. Robert kept out of the way and had no input at all, much to their delight.

Relatives travelled from Lancashire to attend the funeral which took place in the little stone-built church in Gunwalloe Church Cove. It was a most picturesque church situated directly on the beach and welcomed many a tourist through its heavy oak door to Sunday worship. Even dogs were allowed to attend the services. The church was full this very sad day.

The wind howled round the circumference of the old walls, as if mourning the passing of this beautiful lady. The eulogy address was spoken by Uncle John who struggled with his words and that gave everyone a lump in their throat and brought tears to each and every person in the congregation.

Robert sat with Rebecca in the front pew of the church with Grandma and Grandpa next to her, showing a united front on this sad occasion. Rebecca thought, *it must be easier, when you're older, to cope with a death of someone close to you, as Grandpa and Grandma didn't cry, well she never saw them cry. Maybe they did when they were on their own, as she did.*

A couple of days after the funeral, the Catlows together with Rebecca and Rufus, made the long journey back to Lancashire by train. They left Robert, in Cornwall, where he had his new life. There was never much love lost between Marian's parents and Robert Tay, and even more so after the last incident.

After a few days back with her grandparents, Rebecca had started to recharge her batteries. Grandma had fed her good home cooking and the three of them all talked together about the good times and not so good times. They shared their feelings with each other, sitting by the fire in Barbon Street and all felt better for doing so.

Rufus seemed happy enough there with them and loved the open fire and stretched out in front of it blocking any heat for anyone else. It was a new life for him too and now he would always be there to greet Rebecca when she came home from school.

It felt strange to be back at Moonacre without all her friends, but reflecting on her mother's death and comparing it to her current situation, it didn't particularly sadden her. She would finish off this term here and she was sure she would be allowed up to Ford House next term. Matron seemed very supportive of her and explained she would again be given the prefect status, prior to moving up to Ford House the following term.

That cheered Rebecca up and it was something for her to look forward to.

Matron also empathised with her about the death of her mother and told her if ever she needed to talk, or felt unhappy, all she had to do was knock on Matron's door.

She was to be allowed more privileges now she was a prefect and that meant she could see more of Geoff and, hopefully in the holidays, Frankie would visit her at Grandma's. She wasn't looking forward to facing Eddie at school as he was still seeing Pippa Jones. She felt hate towards that girl and still wasn't sorry for clouting her over the head with her satchel. *It was a pity there had been too many witnesses*, she thought!

There was a certain amount of sympathy towards her at school; losing your mum at such a young age was a terrible thing to happen and Rebecca was treated with kid gloves for quite a while.

There was definitely a change in her; she was more sullen and a lot quieter. She was friendly with Bernie at school and the two of them were very into their fell walking and potholing. They participated in every possible walk and caving trip that was available to them and seemed to be mature enough to be given certain responsibilities within the group.

Bernie would give the check talk at the beginning of any ascent or descent and whenever Barry, the head boy, was unavailable, Rebecca would be at the rear of the group acting as last man, much to Eddie's disdain. He was always on the trips and, although they were civil to each other, Rebecca kept herself away from him as much as possible.

He kept trying to involve her in conversations but she was having none of it and any reply needed was abrupt. It was quite an uncomfortable atmosphere when we were all in their company but Rebecca seemed oblivious as if she couldn't care less. She seemed even harder than she was before and it was a relief when she wasn't in our company.

I was getting more confident now with the abseiling and I always had Phillip with me to give me guidance. In fact, I would only go on the trips if Phillip was going.

Potholing was another world underground and the rock formations were stunningly amazing. We are all informed about the conservation message: take nothing but photos and leave nothing but footprints, because potholes and caves are very fragile environments.

As Mr Grey explained to us all, it wasn't just a question of walking, crawling, and slithering, your brain is racing all the time, so concentration is of paramount importance and you have to keep asking yourself questions: How do I do this? How do I conquer the fear that I may never get through it, or under it? or how will I ever get back!? Another thing Mr Grey told us was that you have to find solutions, work out how to push, pull and stretch your body to get through gaps or past obstacles while your mind is telling you the challenges are insurmountable. He went on to say, which I thought was so strange, that one would get into such alien and bloody ridiculous places, that all you could do was dissolve into hysterical laughter. *I don't think I would be laughing too much if that happened to me*, I thought, as I nudged Phillip, and he laughed. I was getting a little cynical and felt I didn't want to carry on any more to attain any higher level with regarding potholing. It definitely wasn't the pastime for me.

CHAPTER 29

Rebecca seemed to be taking her prefect's duties responsibly and she and Matron seemed on a similar wavelength. But I knew Rebecca and knew she was keeping her bread buttered on the right side. All she wanted was to move up into Ford House as soon as possible. She was told the move would be the start of the next term, after the Christmas holidays.

Rebecca was surprised when she saw Pippa Jones walking up the stone steps towards the senior dormitory at Moonacre. She continued up the next flight of stairs which led to the attic and she could hear her rummaging around, moving what sounded like the trunks and suitcases.

She hadn't planned what happened next, but what an ideal opportunity, no witnesses. There was no one around; all were either in prep or watching television, awaiting the supper trolley.

Cautiously and silently, Rebecca turned the key once again in the lock and walked casually back down the stairs, immediately presenting herself in Carr Hall with the others who were telly watching.

No one would hear Pippa's shouting or cries, from the top of the house!

It was about 10 o clock the same evening when the telephone rang in Matron's office informing her that Pippa Jones hadn't arrived back at Ford House after visiting Moonacre. They were getting worried as no one had seen or heard from her.

A search was made of Moonacre and it was Rebecca who informed Matron she could hear shouting coming from the attic. On Matron's instructions, Rebecca ran up the stone steps and unlocked the attic door. She was greeted by Pippa Jones, crying and shivering. She had been locked in the attic for about five hours.

Rebecca cleverly empathised with Pippa and helped her down the stairs to Matron's office. When questioned by Matron, Rebecca said she had seen the attic door wide open earlier in the evening and, as it was the custom that the door should always be kept locked, she locked it; not thinking to check if anyone was actually inside the room.

Pippa was too upset to talk about the incident. Nor could she disprove Rebecca's explanation, but deep down she knew she had locked her in deliberately. Miss Carter drove Pippa back to Ford where she was greeted by some of the girls saying how thankful they were to see her and how unfortunate it was for this to happen.

I remembered being locked in the attic by Rebecca. It was a horrible experience and the memory has stayed with me. As soon as I had heard that Rebecca was involved, I knew it was deliberate and I made it known to Pippa a few days later when she was feeling stronger. I confirmed Pippa's suspicions; this girl must be watched; she was dangerous and couldn't be trusted.

In the meantime, although rumours were rife amongst the girls, that Rebecca had locked Pippa in the attic on purpose, she carried on regardless with her prefect duties.

She was allowed to spend time with Geoff and his family who visited her at school and took her out on exeat days. They saw her at Grandma's house as well, so much so as Grandma and Grandpa approved of the friendship and enjoyed the visits from his family. He was a nice boy and so were his parents. Geoff and his family were useful to Rebecca; anyone could see that.

She was still receiving letters from Frankie who wanted to come and see her. Grandma was not too happy about this and felt Rebecca was being totally disloyal to Geoff. But she didn't want to alienate herself, nor did she wish to upset Rebecca again, so she agreed to let Frankie visit and stay for a few days, in the Christmas holidays.

Rebecca had some juggling to do, but that didn't worry her. She would take Frankie to Blackpool and tell Grandma some cock and bull story about where she would be staying. She had done this before and had survived the animosity when Robert had found out.

She was told by Matron that, after the Christmas holidays, she would be returning to Ford House to join the girls in her year and she was sincerely thanked by Matron for taking her responsibilities as a prefect and performing the tasks well. *Matron wasn't too much of an old stick after all*, she thought. She was happy to be going to Ford next term, it didn't worry her at all that she would be living in the same house as Pippa Jones.

The latter wasn't too pleased and nor was I, I can tell you that!

Rebecca busied herself dragging the old trunk down from the attic and packing everything she had brought with her into the trunk. The laundry bag, containing dirty laundry and her special box was placed at the bottom of the trunk with her clothes, bed blanket spread out over the top of them. Yes, to a happier place for Christmas with Grandma and Grandpa and all Christmas has to bring.

Uncle John had to collect her this Christmas holiday as the girl she normally travelled with was returning to Lagos, Nigeria, where her parents were now working, so all the travelling and collecting from school was done by Uncle John, cousin Betty's father. She loved Uncle John; he was a quiet, unassuming man much like her grandpa and her mum. *Dear Mum*, she thought. How she would miss her this Christmas!

Grandma had done some decorating of the house for Christmas, but the majority had been left to Rebecca to do. She busied herself with the Christmas tree, it always looks more festive when the tree is up and decorated. Some of the tree ornaments were years old. Rebecca remembered them when she was very small as she always decorated the tree. Then there were the paper chains to make. Grandpa helped her make the chains and soon the coloured chains were strung across the living room ceiling, giving the appearance of a rainbow. They all tried to keep happy, even though it was hard to do in the circumstances, as they all missed Marian so much.

Rebecca didn't want to discuss Robert, or where he was to spend Christmas. She hoped she would never see him again. Grandma had pointed out to her, there would be some circumstances when she may have to. Robert had adopted her and was now her legal guardian until she was eighteen years of age. Grandma and Grandpa were unhappy with this also, but said they would have plenty of time, in the coming New Year to hopefully reverse the decision, to make themselves Rebecca's legal guardians.

In the meantime, he was still paying the school fees, thankfully.

They wouldn't let this problem spoil their Christmas.

Rebecca was a great help to Grandma with all the shopping for Christmas. All the family were getting together on Christmas Day and on Boxing Day they were all going to cousin Betty's house. Rebecca loved the family celebrations and it would help each and every one of them to be cheerful in spite of them all missing Marian.

Christmas Eve was a hive of activity in the Catlow kitchen.

The Christmas cake and pudding had been made in November, but the cake was to be iced and decorated this Christmas Eve by Rebecca. The stuffing was homemade and smelt delicious as Grandma stuffed the turkey in preparation for putting it in the oven first thing in the morning.

There were all the vegetables to prepare, to make life easier on Christmas Day and a new batch of mince pies to make, as Grandpa had devoured most of the first lot Grandma had made.

It would be Christmas Day in the morning and there were presents to open, a very exciting time. She was surprised to see a large parcel, wrapped in brown paper addressed to her. It had been put under the window along with all the other gifts but it stood out because it was the only one wrapped in brown paper and was amongst all the others wrapped in Christmas paper. The postmark said Blackpool.

Rufus was also excited at all the hustle and bustle going on, always standing, wagging his tail hoping for a titbit. He was very mischievous and insisted on dragging streamers out of the decoration box and leaving them strewn all of the floor. He was so funny and had them all collapsing in laughter, good old Rufus!

Once all the preparations were done it was time to settle down for Christmas Eve nibbles in front of the roaring fire and watching Grandma's favourite shows on the television. Rebecca still had her presents to wrap. She had bought everyone a small gift, even Rufus had a doggy selection box. So, she carefully wrapped the gifts sitting at the large table in the parlour.

She was very inquisitive as to what was in the brown paper parcel but Grandpa had forbidden her to open it as it wasn't yet Christmas Day. She knew it was from Eddie; she could tell from the writing and was somewhat surprised to actually receive anything from him, after leaving each other in sad circumstances and a relationship in tatters. She had heard a whisper from Charlotte Jackson who had told her Eddie was sorry he had two-timed her and wanted to go back with her at the beginning of the next term. She was comforted by this news and hoped that it would happen, even though she still had Geoff and Frankie in tow. She wouldn't do anything too drastic just yet and decided to let circumstances take their own course. It would be sorted out in the very near future, one way or another.

Everyone arrived on Christmas Day morning at the same time. They had hired a taxi which was to return to collect them at about ten o'clock that evening. They were all dressed in their best clothes; cousin Betty had a red and black dress on in a velvet material and she looked gorgeous as it complemented her dark hair. Everyone was in the Christmas spirit and it wasn't long before they all were all sitting around the fire and opening their Christmas gifts, partaking of a glass of sherry and glass of ale.

Rebecca loved all her gifts ranging from underwear and toiletries to a new jumper and a very up-to-date shift dress from cousin Betty and it fitted perfectly. She kept the brown paper parcel until the last. Eddie had done her proud and it would appear he had spent quite a bit of money on her. It was a beautiful, outdoor, quilted jacket, perfect for going up the mountains and potholing. It was red, edged in black and fitted her like a glove. It was so warm and very trendy. She was over the moon and couldn't wait to wear it. She must really try to forgive him now. The thought went through her mind, *I bet he never bought Pippa Jones a present.* Rebecca was happy!

She had also received gifts from Geoff and Frankie.

Frankie had given her a gold necklace, a souvenir from Gibraltar, where he had been on assignment over the last few weeks before Christmas. He was at home now with his family in London for a few days but suggested that he would like to visit Rebecca at Grandma's, after Christmas.

Geoff had given her a poncho, which his mother had crocheted; all the colours complementing Rebecca's blonde hair in beiges, browns, and gold. Ponchos were very trendy and it was the first one Rebecca had ever had. It would go beautifully with her high leg brown leather boots which Grandma and Grandpa had given her for Christmas.

She was very happy with all the gifts; she would try everything on and look in the mirror when everyone had gone home and then decide what to wear tomorrow when they were going to cousin Betty's.

The rest of Christmas Day was spent eating Grandma's sumptuous roast turkey dinner, accompanied by clove-infused ham with a honey glaze; it was an amazing dinner. Uncle John found the sixpence in the Christmas pudding and pressed it in Rebecca's hand under the table.

Then it was time for Grandpa to get on the 'old Joanna.' This is what Rebecca loved: all of them singing along to the old songs which Grandpa played. She could see his hands weren't as nimble as they used to be and that arthritis was making them stiff and causing lumps on the end of his fingers. But the exercise playing the piano keyboards probably gave them a good workout. *He should play more often so as to keep them more nimble*, she thought.

She laughed to herself when she watched him pick up a bottle of beer from the crate next to the piano and, with each bottle consumed, Grandma had her beady eyes on him. 'Go easy, Willie,' she would say. But it was Christmas Day so he could ignore her.

Rebecca went up to bed about midnight. She helped Grandma clear the table and wash up all the pots and drinks glasses after everyone had left.

She drifted off to sleep, eventually. Rufus lay by her bed which comforted her. She remembered in the dark, when her mum and she had shared the bedroom before Robert came along, and thought about how quickly things change. She so missed her mum.

Everything in the room was still the same, even the sound of the hot water cylinder filling up. And then she went to sleep.

CHAPTER 30

Rebecca had decided after Christmas that she would telephone Frankie and tell him she couldn't see him before she returned to school. He wasn't too happy with this information and the phone call ended when he slammed the phone down on her.

She had blamed her grandma and family commitments but of course he didn't believe her. She wasn't unduly worried. It was either seeing Frankie and visiting Blackpool, which was a bit risky as she might bump into Eddie, or going with Drew and his friends on New Year's Eve to the all-nighter, on the other side of town.

There was no competition, the all-night party won hands down.

She informed grandma she was staying at Drew's house. That was the plan anyway. Drew's parents were away again so Grandma couldn't check with them.

Cousin Betty's present came in very useful. The dress had cutaway sleeves and buttoned up the front. It was a maroon colour with specks of pinks and reds in the pattern. She also wore her maroon patent wedge heel shoes for dancing in. She looked at herself in the mirror, her hair cropped quite short on her forehead, she looked a proper mod now in every way.

Drew was pleased to see her and they chatted away at

Grandma's before they set off to Drew's house where they were meeting his friends.

Grandma was happy enough she was with Drew, a very sensible boy who would look after Rebecca. He was now driving as well; his parents had bought him a Mini Traveller estate car, which was most useful. Now they could travel in the car to the all-night club, instead of catching the bus. She wondered if Ricky would be there. H might well be, as he travelled far and wide to the all-nighters. That's what the mods did; they travelled, if it was a good scene.

The Bird Trap wasn't too far away; just in the next town. Rebecca had been before. There were seven of them in Drew's car, two were curled up in the boot and the others squashed in on the seats. Everyone was in a great mood. They all had New Year drinks at Drew's before they left, so all were a little tipsy, apart from Drew who took his driving very seriously.

Once again, the queue to enter the club was stretching up the street to the main road. There was much exuberance amongst the revellers and the music was yet again blasting out into the late evening air, much to the annoyance of the residents in the same street. They were still attempting to get the club closed for good.

She stayed with Drew and his friends and danced with them nearly all of the night. She was pleased to see Ricky on the dance floor, doing his dance and spinning around on his own. She went over to say hello, but he looked at her as if she was a stranger. She could see his pupils dilated and he just wasn't a part of the real world. He looked thinner as well. He was totally ambivalent towards her and that made her sad. Not angry, just

247

seeing him like that made her realise she would not be part of this whole scene involving the drug taking; look what it had done to Ricky. He was on a downward slope; she could see that. He did not realise who she was, so she left the dance floor and joined Drew and his friends again. This had saddened her.

She then saw Ricky fall over on the dance floor and he wasn't moving; he just lay still. A crowd surrounded him, then there were cries of, 'Phone an ambulance.' Poor Ricky was taken off to hospital. She hoped he would be alright as he hadn't looked at all well. She probably would never know.

The happy New Year's Eve had turned sour and it was decided the club should close its doors earlier that the normal seven o'clock.

It was still very dark outside and it had been raining, but the in-crowd made their way to where Drew's car was parked, all chatting about Ricky. There was nowhere open for breakfast, so it was all back to Drew's house for a fry-up. All of them were ravenous and exhausted.

Rebecca managed to sleep for a few hours before heading off with Drew back to Grandma's.

It was a sad end to the old year and a sad beginning to the New Year. *Things must get better*, she thought.

The rest of the Christmas holidays went quickly.

Geoff had written to her and she had replied, saying she looked forward to seeing him when she was back at school and maybe he would like to come up for the next exeat day. That reply would placate him and his mother for a few weeks, she decided.

It was exciting driving with Uncle John into the driveway of Ford House.

Grandma had come along for the ride, and it gave them the chance to look around the new boarding house. They were most impressed with the divan beds and their wooden headboards. There was a pink cover over Rebecca's bed and lovely new, soft pillows. A great contrast to Moonacre, with its iron bedheads and frames.

Rebecca was on the top floor of the house; all the new girls started there. Her bed was under a small window which overlooked the fields and road at the side of the house. There were three other older girls in her room and the other girls from her year shared another room.

Pippa Jones and her friends occupied the large first-floor bedroom. She was one of the first girls back at Ford after the holiday and that gave her chance to have a proper look around the place and unpack her trunk once again.

Rebecca couldn't have been more pleasant with me when I saw her. I was in another room on the same floor. I was also one of the first to return. She was treating me like I was her best friend, but that didn't cut, I had been trampled on by Rebecca so many times when it suited her.

I was under no illusion, it was she, who was the new girl now. Bernie, Charlotte, and Helena all still seemed pals with her, judging from the laughter and storytelling of the holidays.

She was very vocal about her present from Eddie and I am sure the information was received on the first floor. There was always someone ready to squeal to the senior girls to keep in their good books.

They all walked down to school together that first morning, skipping and jumping around, and there was excitement to see the boys. Even I was excited to see my Phillip again. I had spent time with him in the holidays, which was wonderful, but still couldn't wait to see him.

Bernie was still seeing Pete, Charlotte had a boyfriend too, but I didn't know him, she didn't speak of him often. She wisely kept some things to herself.

It would be interesting to see what was going to happen with the saga of Pippa, Rebecca, and Eddie and who would win the catch! The catch being Eddie.

There was a big crowd surrounding the tuck shop at the morning's first break. Everyone seemed to be talking at once, with so much to say to each other, about Christmas and what they had all done. Pippa and her friends were there also, but standing slightly apart from Rebecca's crowd.

Eddie and Pete were together and made their way over to Rebecca and Bernie who were in a crowd of about ten other girls.

I observed the conversation between Eddie and Rebecca seemed strained, although they carried on talking to each other most of the break, much to the disgust of Pippa Jones, who didn't look too happy. Eddie appeared not to notice Pippa, who was gaining some attention from another boy who was in the sixth form. She was doing her damnedest to get his attention, looking over in Eddie's direction as she was flirting with the boy. Eddie seemed oblivious to Pippa Jones and it would appear, according to Rebecca, that their relationship was back on the track and they were an item again.

Phillip confirmed this to me and said that Eddie had been worried all over the Christmas break that Rebecca wouldn't want to see him ever again.

I thought, he must be delusional; he could get any girl he wanted!

Life at Ford House seemed to be a much more relaxing than Moonacre.

Well, it was warmer and some of the rooms had carpets on the floor, which was a real luxury compared to the bare floorboards of Moonacre.

The food also, made by Mrs Prindle, the cook, was gorgeous; real homemade food tasting just like home.

There was not a housemistress at Ford, just Matron, who was a very pleasant lady. Her name was Miss Bea and she wore tweed skirts. Her hair was grey, cut short, and you could tell she wasn't married. She was very old-fashioned. Her vocabulary consisted of, 'Good gracious', 'Good Lord' and 'Good grief', when surprised. Rebecca could mimic her to a 'T.' We nicknamed her 'The Bee'. And, when she became annoyed, we said 'The Bee is out to sting', and when she was doing her rounds, we used to say, 'The Bee is a-buzzing'. Rebecca then would say, 'and her hair is a fuzzing.'

That gave us all the giggles, I think she was becoming a bit deaf as some things she didn't hear, but maybe that was her choice. For Matron to be a little hard of hearing worked perfectly for us girls.

The midnight wanderings had commenced. The fire escape door from the first-floor bedroom was the means of exit. Much easier access to the dark moonlit nights than having to slide down the kitchen roof at Moonacre. The key to this was in a small glass case, fixed onto the wall next to the fire escape door. On close inspection, one could see how the screws had been loosened with each attempt and the plaster work was flaking from the wall.

It became obvious that the key was constantly being taken to unlock the door so another method must be adopted. Luck was on our side. Another key was found, by pure chance. A day boy, with a group of his friends climbed the fire escape metal ladder in the pitch black and just happened to try the key of his cafe, where he lived in a nearby village and … guess what?… it fitted perfectly, and opened the fire escape door!

This was copied and we now had our own key, so no more unscrewing the fixture on the wall. The key must be guarded and it was kept hidden by one the older girls. Very few knew who held the key. Us girls on the top floor were not privilege to this information, but Rebecca made her business to find out, one way or another. She remarked, 'One place it isn't, is in the *Big Bumper Book for Girls*, and we all laughed; even Bernie saw the funny side of this remark.

Rebecca definitely started to use Bernie as a confidante as they seemed as thick as thieves. No more fighting between them. In fact, they seemed to stand up for each other. All the past animosity was swept under the carpet. Pete and Eddie were mates and so were Bernie and Rebecca. It actually made for perfect harmony when we were all together. Only Pippa Jones was the problem for Rebecca and of course my feelings hadn't changed either; I was still very wary of her.

Pippa Jones had started to go out with the sixth form boy. His name was Craig. He was a local day pupil which meant he was not restricted to boarding protocol as we all were. He lived in High Brantham and could come and go as he pleased. We all knew he used to meet Pippa around the back of Ford House in the early evening. You could peep at them, snogging each other, leaning up against the wall. Sometimes, some of the girls would pour water on them from the bedroom above and then scarper. Then they had to move their position a few times until they ended up at the back of the garage or wood shed.

One early evening, Rebecca was on clearing-up duty after dinner. She was in the larder room, replacing food in the tins and in the large fridge. This small room was situated next to the general purpose room which housed outdoor coats, ironing boards, and sports equipment. It also housed the back door, which opened onto the large garden at the back of the house.

Rebecca pricked up her ears, when she heard Pippa's voice. She was talking to her friend Penny Hodge. Quietly spoken Pippa said,' Need the key tonight, Pen.'

Bingo! Rebecca thought. So, Penny Hodge had had it all the time.

It had to be one of the girls who went out at night and Penny did regularly. She too had a boyfriend in the village who had a car, which was most convenient for her. She could slip out, into the car and no one would see her. We had to keep to the fields and paths, away from any main roads, so no one could report us. Matron couldn't hear us, as she was definitely going deaf and once our bedroom lights were out, there was no more checking if our beds were occupied.

Now Rebecca knew where the key was, it was only a matter of time before she put her new plan into operation. It was called, 'Get the Pippa plan.' All she had to do was find the key amongst Penny's belongings and hopefully get it copied.

She took her opportunity one Saturday morning. She feigned a headache when all the girls were off to shop in High Brantham. This is generally what happened on a Saturday morning. The girls all wore their mufti clothes, but had to wear a uniform coat or the blazer over the top, to walk to the village.

She found the key almost immediately. *How pathetic*, she thought, *what a stupid place to hide it!* It was bound to be under Penny's mattress somewhere and there it was, under her mattress by her pillows, resting on the slats of the bedframe. She didn't take it then, as she needed to get it copied and they would probably miss it this weekend. She would wait until mid-week and get another copy done by one of the day boys.

She was happy her plan was coming along nicely.

She and Bernie met the boys in the afternoon. They sat in the back of the chip shop in High Brantham, drinking hot Horlicks with frothy milk and eating chips with plenty of salt and vine-gar on them. The four of them discussed the next potholing outing and Rebecca enthused to Eddie how much she loved her Christmas present from him. She didn't get him a present! All afternoon was spent in the back of the chippy and they ate a few bags of chips. Saturday tea wasn't great at Ford, as cook took Saturdays off, so they had to fill up before tea.

The next Saturday they were off with the caving group to Lost John's cave and were all looking forward to it. Rebecca could wear her new jacket and spend all day with Eddie. Out of all her boyfriends, Eddie was always the special one.

We couldn't hear if the older girls went out that night as we were at the top of the house and the door to their landing on the first floor was always closed at night. However, we could certainly tell who had been gallivanting the following morning by the tired eyes looking around the breakfast tables, still covered in their eye makeup, which wasn't allowed anyway. They were lethargic most of the Sunday and by that, I mean Penny and Pippa. They even cancelled their Sunday walk.

When the coast was clear at the beginning of the week, Rebecca seized her opportunity and took the key, which was still in the same place under Penny's mattress and secreted it in her satchel before she walked down to school. She must get it copied as soon as possible and made the arrangements with the day boy whose parents owned the cafe in the village to get it done.

He liked Rebecca and she could manipulate him. He even paid for the copying of the key and was sworn to secrecy, which he was most happy with and felt privileged to be brought in as her confidant.

The following day she had the two keys in her possession. She even bought the boy chocolate from the tuck shop. Eddie was most surprised and said jokingly 'Why did you do that Rebecca, what about me?' Rebecca just touched her finger to her nose and didn't explain. She took her opportunity to replace the key under Penny's mattress during prep time. All the girls were in the dining room doing their homework and she just made an excuse to leave the room. It only took her a few seconds and she was back with her head stuck in her books. No one had missed the key and it was now back in its safe place.

Rebecca kept the other one, for *her* rainy days!

It all happened too quickly the coming week for Rebecca to put her plan into operation. Her intention was to secrete the key in Pippa's dressing table drawers for the powers that be to find it in a search of the rooms. The headmistress had information some girls were leaving Ford in the middle of the night probably via the fire escape door.

It was the demise for Pippa and Penny, as they were caught returning up the fire escape steps into the first-floor bedroom at 4 am, by Matron and the local policeman; Pippa carrying the key in her hand.

The maintenance man had discovered that the key in the glass case on the wall had been tampered with and the screws were loose in the wall. He had reported this to Matron and she had informed the headmistress. This resulted in the local policeman keeping observations on the outside of Ford and saw the girls returning, running up the driveway.

There was a real commotion to say the least. The crying and noise woke up the whole house. We could only surmise what was occurring down on the first floor, but we had a good idea.

The same morning at breakfast, the rumours were flying.

There were two girls missing from breakfast so one hadn't to be a genius as to what had happened during the night. Rebecca was quietly smug and said, 'It couldn't have happened to a better person.'

The girls were never seen again; both were told to pack their bags and they left the school the same way as Harry, when she had been kicked out.

Just one key left now!

Rebecca hadn't planned these recent developments so she was quietly relieved with the outcome. That was Pippa out of the way, she was no longer any threat.

She was content.

Caving had been cancelled for the forthcoming Saturday as it was exeat day on the Sunday. It was rescheduled for the following Saturday.

Rebecca was a little disappointed but there was always exeat day to look forward to as she had planned to visit Harry at her home.

Harry's dad was going to collect her from the school gates after church and take her out for lunch as they had done previously, before that fateful day when Tony had died. He drove the same way home and they passed the exact spot where Tony came off his bike.

On arrival at Harry's everyone was hugging each other. There were people there Rebecca didn't know, it was some sort of celebration and Rebecca only found out it was a homecoming for Harry's mum.

Rebecca and Harry jumped around and hugged each other as they were so pleased to be together again and today, they could talk and laugh just like they used to and make up for lots of lost time.

Harry's mum had been on a long cruise, away for over a month and the family were giving her a welcome home party. Her mum looked very tanned and walked around with a cigarette in a long cigarette holder. She was a very glamorous lady.

Rebecca loved it at Harry's, it was so exciting. There were lots of friends there, all sipping champagne and dressed in their cocktail dresses.

Rebecca had her dress which cousin Betty had bought her and felt very grown up amongst all the Bowen family and their friends.

Lunch was at the local hotel in the village all within walking distance from Harry's house. Rebecca had been there previously, when she had enjoyed sipping white wine with her lunch. Everyone enjoyed the carvery, served in a special room overlooking the Kent estuary. They finished the three-course meal before sauntering back down the road to the party room in Harry's house. The occasion was no doubt, going to extend into the evening as no one was ready to leave and there were many more corks-a-popping.

However, both Rebecca and Harry's brother, who was still at the school, had to return, so it was with sadness Rebecca said her farewells to everyone. She missed Harry a lot and they had not made any arrangements to visit each other in the near future, which saddened both girls. She had had a wonderful day and re-lived the whole time as they drove along the country roads back to Brantham, arriving just in time for supper.

She thanked Harry's dad very much for a lovely day and for

driving her back to Ford. He was a lovely gentle person and there was always the thought in Rebecca's head saying,' Why couldn't my mum have married Mr Bowen?'

CHAPTER 31

A few weeks into the term Rebecca received refreshing news in a letter from Grandma. Her legal adoption had been transferred from Robert to Grandma and Grandpa. She was so happy now that Robert Tay was out of her life. She never wished to set eyes on him again. It was what she had been praying for and now she need not have anything more to do with him. He even agreed to carry on paying the school fees. Grandma and Grandpa were also ecstatic with the news and they sent her a copy of her new birth certificate. It was still in the name of Tay, but Rebecca accepted this, as there was nothing she could do about it. She was very happy now, and, things seemed to be going her way. Pippa Jones was no longer in the equation and not a threat to her and Eddie anymore.

However, there was a rumour circulating that it was Rebecca who split on the girls that night which led to them being caught. We will never know but if that was the case, it was unforgivable. That would be just like her to inform on them.

She and Bernie still seemed as thick as thieves, but I knew this was only for one reason; on Bernie's part that is related to the saying: 'Keep your friends close but keep your enemies closer still.'

The pull of the night air for these two girls was almost too much to bear. They both so wanted to escape the drudgery of the boarding house and feel free amongst the fields and of course to be able to meet Pete and Eddie. It was because of this and due to a question from Bernie about how were they to get out in the first place that Rebecca foolishly divulged she had another key for the fire escape door which was hidden amongst her belongings.

This was music to Bernie's ears and, armed with this information, she shared it with Belinda Rudd, a prefect at Ford. The last thing Belinda wanted was more trouble at Ford and for them all to be gated and lose any privileges they may have. So, it was decided that a search was to be made of Rebecca's room and her belongings at a convenient time when Rebecca was away from Ford House. The search was scheduled for the coming weekend when the cavers were on their expedition to Lost John's cave, an outing Rebecca would not want to miss.

Belinda was very careful to keep this information to herself and thanked Bernie for trusting it to her. Both girls must keep this information very private so as not to lose the duplicate key.

The caving group were up very early on the Saturday morning and that included me, Bernie, Rebecca and Charlotte. We had an early breakfast of porridge and scrambled eggs on toast. Belinda wasn't part of the group this day. All our kit was assembled together the night before and we checked it all through with each other. This procedure was done automatically, prior to any caving outings, as it was so important we all had the proper equipment with us.

The last-minute stuff to put in our bags were flasks of tea and sandwiches. We laughed together as none of us had Miss Cross's staple diet of a Rich Tea biscuit; instead, it now included an orange Club biscuit.

The bus collected us. The boys were already on the back seat of the coach shouting at us to join them. I was very pleased to see Phillip as he said he hadn't felt too well the day before. I just prayed he would be there as I couldn't back out of the trip. We were on our way to Leck Fell and to tackle Lost John's Cave. We had been there before but this time we were entering the pot via a different entrance.

We followed the stream on Leck Fell to the main entrance of the pot. We had a good day for our walk, it was a little misty up on the fell but that hopefully would soon clear. Everyone was in a cheery mood and we couldn't wait to abseil down the pot to be encompassed by the beautiful underground colours and caverns. I was again supported by Phillip; he always could tell I was apprehensive.

Rebecca seemed to take it all in her stride and she had become most competent, I had to admit.

There were about twelve of us in the group this day. Mr Grey was pleased with the turnout. Barry, the head boy, was also there, bringing up the rear as usual. Rebecca and Eddie were also at the rear of the group assisting Barry. We all managed the abseil down into the pot. It was very narrow in parts and I had to breathe in several times to cram my body down the small gaps between the rocks. It opened out on the floor of the pot, a drop of roughly sixty feet and room for us all to gather together.

Our next task was to walk along the undulating crevice between the rocks, which was already running with a good amount of water which was swirling around. Absence of surface drainage on the moorland, no tree cover, and only patches of heather resulted in a subterranean drainage network. After a few hundred yards the stream fell into a large translucent pool which was also swirling around.

There was a shaft of light directly onto the pool, it was most beautiful and we stood admiring its formations. There was only one way forward and that was through the pool. I was hesitant as we did not know its depth but Mr Grey assured us it wouldn't be above waist height. *Help*, I thought as I wasn't expecting to get wet through. I just followed and said nothing as Rebecca was again giving directions from the rear of the group and taking it all in her stride.

The water was ice cold, it was nearly spring and all the ice from the surrounding streams and fells was melting, hence the freezing water. We all waded through the pool which was about ten feet across and about four feet in depth. The floor of the pool was full of rocks but with our sturdy boots that wasn't a problem. I was elated to get through to the other side and received a pat on the back from Phillip. I wished I could have celebrated with a cup of hot tea but I would have to wait until we reached the other end of the gully. I felt most uncomfortable and vowed to myself then and there I would not be putting myself through this again, for love nor money!

This would be my last descent.

Our next commitment on the trail was a connection called The Tube. It was frightening to say the least and I was sure I wouldn't be able to cope, shuffling along on my belly with my head turned on one side. If I wasn't claustrophobic before, I certainly would be if I survived this encounter. I had noticed the water beneath my feet was rising. I wasn't unduly worried at first but then I heard the sounds of water in the pot amplify. It gurgled loudly as it raced around the rocks to where I was standing. I had to go forward and attempt to crawl through the small space between the rocks to the next cave. There was no returning to the pool we had walked through.

Mr Grey seemed concerned and immediately took control and gave instructions as to how we should conquer this long narrow crawl between the two rocks. He didn't wish to panic anyone but stated the water was rising and we had to get through to the other side. He said it was a flash flood, but we *were* aware that this could happen at any time.

However, we were unaware the heavens above us had opened and the rain was torrential. One by one, we shimmied our way between the gap in the rocks and thankfully made it to the other side with Phillip, who finally pulled me through, as the water rose. We were the last to come through the narrow crevice. My heart was in my mouth all the way and I could hear it beating ten to the dozen. I was frightened and hoped I could crawl through the crevice before the water beat me to it.

I heard Rebecca's voice behind me. I couldn't really make out what she was saying because of the noise of the water. Her voice sounded loud and muffled, as if she was trying to shout above the noise of the water. She was behind me, bringing up the rear as she often did. I thought Barry and Eddie were behind her but when I eventually got through the gap, I saw them with the others. They all had anxious looks on their faces. Rebecca *was* behind me, bringing up the rear.

I never spoke of this and I gazed at Phillip as he stared back at me. I lowered my eyes.

Rebecca never emerged from the tube and the water was

264

flowing through the rocks, meaning the void at the start of the crawl must be full of water by now. We were all numb. She wasn't with us and I never spoke.

The search of Rebecca's room and belongings at Ford House had been completed by Belinda. At the bottom of her laundry bag were found several items, which couldn't be explained: the key was found; and Bernie's ear phone, which had been cut, was also there. It was a mystery as to what the other items were. Belinda would have to wait until Rebecca arrived back at Ford and listen to her explanation regarding the contents of the laundry bag.

There was no doubt in Belinda's mind that Rebecca had a lot of explaining to do and she would interrogate her when she returned that evening from caving. She obviously was unaware of the tragedy occurring in the depths of Lost John's Pot and therefore the contents of the laundry bag would sadly never be explained.

The water arrived in torrents and the chasm filled up so fast that, unless you were able to get through to the other side of the tube, you would not have stood a chance.

The water enveloped her.

Her head is pounding and every cell in her body is screaming for oxygen. She keeps fighting the weight of the water and extreme cold, until she feels like her head is going to explode. She has to take a breath.

So, she does and for some reason it doesn't hurt like she thought it would. She is not scared anymore; actually, it's almost peaceful. She begins to fall. She falls further and further into the darkness until it swallows her whole.

No more anxiety, no more cold, no more water. Just a kind, helping hand from Mum, as she emerges into the sunlight.

I never did venture down a cave again. I never spoke of Lost John's cave and of that fateful day to anyone; not even Phillip.

Phillip and I were married the year after we left Brantham and I became a farmer's wife. I carry this burden with me to this day. I had no love for the girl who used to make me laugh and later make me cry but she lived by her own rules and she hurt others along the way.

'What goes around comes around,' Grandma Catlow always used to tell her.

Acknowledgements

My thanks to friends, Linda, who assisted me with the editing, Alan, for his support and who gave me directions regarding potholing and caving and Martin, who is always there for me with help and sound advice. My gratitude and thanks to James at The Conrad Press.

ACKNOWLEDGMENTS

About the Author

The author, Susan Janet Roach Douglas née Smith, attended boarding school in Yorkshire during the 1960s. This is Susan's second novel, the first entitled *Our wee Geordie* published in 2016, is a novel based on a true story about an unruly Belfast boy. Susan worked as a police officer both in the Lancashire Constabulary and later in London's Metropolitan Police, where she joined the Criminal Investigation Department in 1982. Her career spanned thirty years. After her retirement, she and her husband went to live in Scotland where they ran a guest house in the highlands for a number of years and where she wrote her first novel. Sadly, Susan's husband became terminally ill so they returned to Northern Ireland, where he passed away in 2016. Susan still lives in Northern Ireland with her Labrador, Laddie, where she enjoys long walks by the Irish sea and the occasional glass of wine.